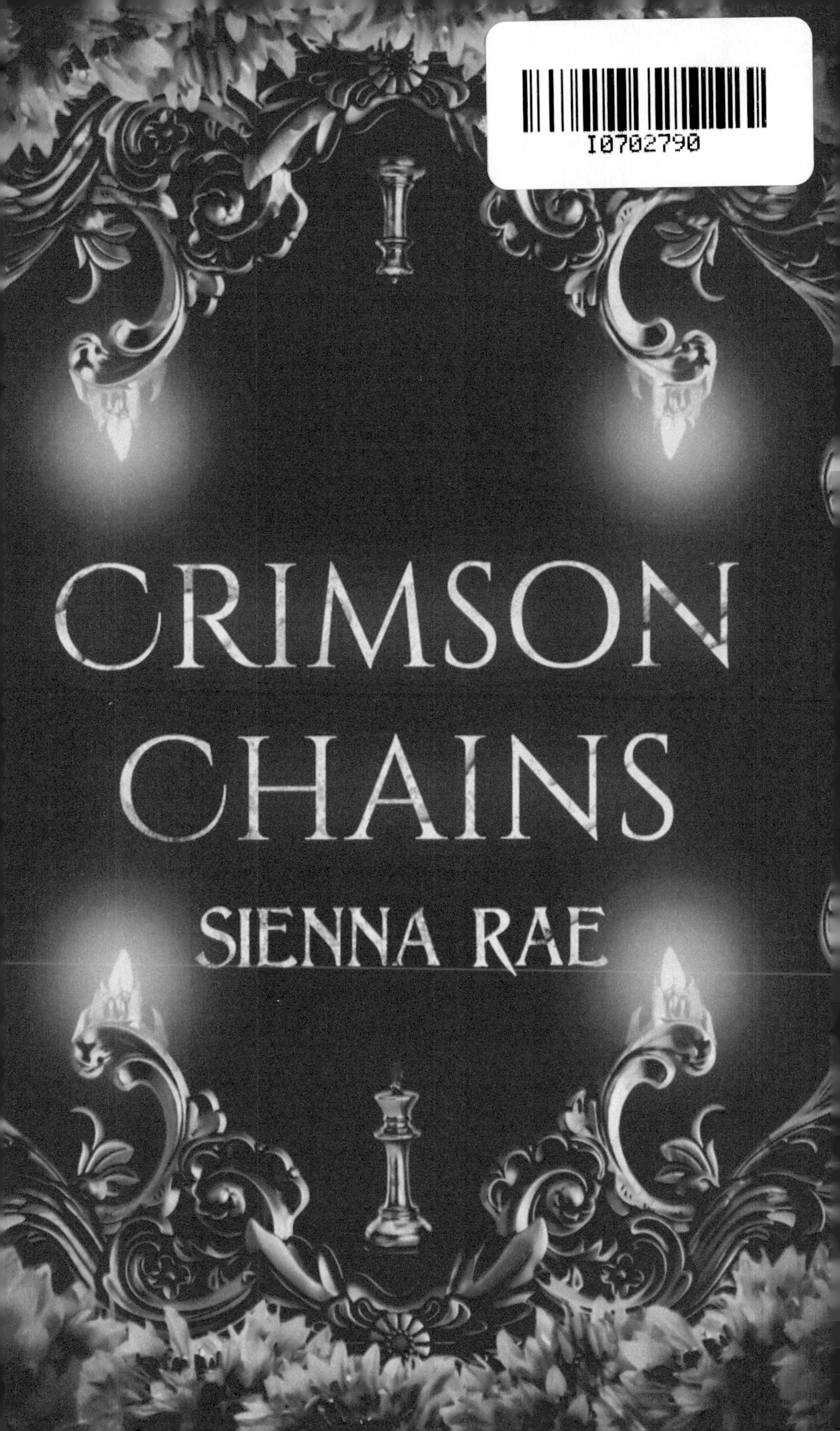

CRIMSON
CHAINS
SIENNA RAE

CONTENT WARNING

<u>The book you are about to read is a paranormal horror and contains material that may not be suitable for all audiences. Please consider your mental health and read at your own risk.</u>
<u>18+ Material</u>

Profanity
Death of a Family Member
Mentions of Domestic Violence
Mentions of Child Abuse
Abuse of Pill Medication
Descriptions of Bodily Fluids
Descriptive Gore
Sexism
Cannibalism
Forced Cannibalism
Blood Drinking
Mutilation
Torture

CONTENT WARNING

Suicide
Psychological Torment
Starvation
Piquerism
Stalking
Exsanguination
Skinning
Suffocation

National Suicide Prevention

IF YOU OR SOMEONE YOU KNOW IS IN CRISIS:

Call the National Suicide Prevention Lifeline at
1-800-273-TALK (8255), or
text the Crisis Text Line (Text HELLO to 741741).

For confidential support available 24/7 for everyone in the United States, call 988.

Please call 911 if someone if there is an emergency.

OFFICIAL CRIMSON CHAINS PLAYLIST

She Wants Revenge- Tear You Apart

Chapter Six:
Secession Studios, Greg Dombrowski- Heart of Darkness

Chapter Seven:
Secession Studios, Greg Dombrowski- Lucidity

Chapter Eight:
Secession Studios, Greg Dombrowski- V Is For Villain

Chapter Nine:
Puscifer- The Remedy

Chapter Ten:
Lorna Shore- Into the Earth

Chapter Eleven:
Secession Studios, Greg Dombrowski- Requiem

Chapter Twelve:
UNSECRET, Neoni- Fallout
Luca Francini- You Will Never Keep Me Down

Chapter Thirteen:
Cradle of Filth- Hallowed Be Thy Name
Mikko Tarmia- Theme for Unknown

Chapter Fourteen:
Secession Studios, Greg Dombrowski- Methods of Madness
Breaking Benjamin- So Cold
Two Steps from Hell, Thomas Bergersen- Heart

Chapter Fifteen:
Eternal Eclipse- Afterlight

Chapter Sixteen:
Slayer- Delusions of Saviour

Chapter Seventeen:
Whitechapel- When a Demon Defiles a Witch
Lorna Shore- Pain Remains Part 1

Chapter Eighteen:
Disturbed- Unstoppable
Otep- Battle Ready
Lamb of God- To The Grave
Luca Francini- Juggernaut
Secession Studios- Darkness of Light

*To the people who tried to destroy me and my spirit,
you forgot that a Phoenix rises from its ashes*

PROLOGUE

Panic overtakes me as I race my way to safety out of this dense forest. Stumbling over fallen branches and condensed underbrush, a cacophony of obnoxious noises opens a path for my foreign enemy to find me. A string of profanity worsens my situation as twigs and jagged rocks slice my legs and pierce the bottom of my bare feet. Tiny stings burn along my sliced flesh. I'm not sure who or what is out there, but I can feel their haunting presence—an uncomfortable caress creeps up my spine and tangles around my limbs.

"Get the fuck away from me," I shout back to unseen ears.

Listening intently beyond the noises of my stampeding feet and gasping breaths, I notice no sounds are coming from any direction, a void of nothingness— a creatureless wooden

"

wasteland devoid of life. Briefly pausing my steps, my head pivots on a swivel for any movement or sound approaching. Despite the fact I can't hear what is out there doesn't mean it has given up and stopped chasing me. Uncertain of my safest path, I bolt off desperately to the right. Fear-laced adrenaline courses powerfully in my veins, driving my body to the brink of exhaustion.

The full moon rests high up in the sky, but its illumination barely pierces through the thick canopy of leaves hovering over the forest. The nightly effervescent glow from the next town over can barely be seen permeating the tree-line—another useless light source. Every hair on my body stands at attention and goose bumps pepper my skin. *Must keep running*, I yell internally. Wheezing choked breaths squeeze in my chest cavity, searching for relief and begging to end this strain. Pushing my body beyond its physical limits is the only way to survive whatever is after me. Throbbing blood flow is the one sound loud enough to penetrate to the deep recesses of my eardrums and crack through the terror. My heartbeat thumps relentlessly against my ribcage, constricting and tightening around each gulp of air. With visibility limited, I put all of my faith in my limbs propelling me forward. Step by agonizing step the muscles begin to twist and contort in knots running up my legs. *Fuck!*

Absent visibility is the perfect recipe for a disastrous collision with the unknown. *Crack!* One misstep and my shin slams violently against a fallen tree. Immediately my body is sent tumbling to the ground, failing immensely in an attempt to extend my arms out in front of my falling frame. An electrifying shockwave of pain sets off every nerve ending firing through my system when I collide with the cold forest floor. Upon impact, the air that was attempting to expand my struggling lungs became nonexistent—stolen from me with no sign of returning.

I can feel the frightening entity begin to close the gap between us. Disorientation blankets me momentarily. *Get up, stupid, get up.* Tangled under and around tree roots, my escape plan is fleeting away by the second. Regardless of what my lungs and cramping muscles say, I have to keep pushing. Scrambling to get my arms out from underneath my torso, the internal censors of my frayed nervous system paralyze me with fear.

The ominous looming presence found its path to me.

I've always been told that the best moments of your life are supposed to flash through your mind seconds before your death.

Bang. Bang. Bang.

I

"Rayna, open up, it's me," Jack shouts through my apartment door.

I shoot up in bed, my lungs screaming for relief. It felt so real, they always feel so real. Suffering from night terrors is nothing new to me, however, I've come to assume their pattern. I'd go months without a single disturbance and then, out of nowhere, my dreamscape barrier would crack beyond repair, leaving the portal wide open for my terrors to return. In the past, they've thankfully only lasted three days at a time, but I still can't figure out their cause or trigger. Unfortunately, this present recurring night terror sequence is lasting far longer than three days. The repetition of the unyielding panic-stricken chase makes it especially unnerving. Always running and invariably falling as I am caught by my mysterious foe. I'm not sure how far this nightmare would have taken me if Jack hadn't shaken me from its grasp. His voice and his strength are the lifeline from the hellscape —my bottled emotions, the tormentor.

The most unsettling aspect is how eerily familiar my dense forest prison appears to me. Its unearthliness seeps a cold breath through my skin, burrowing deeply into my bones. I've traveled there previously, except the details and location escape me.

"I know you're home, open your door," he calls out again while giving my front door another three knocks. Always three times, nothing more, nothing less.

The last thing I want is to deal with him right now. Granted, he seems to be the only one keeping my head on straight these days, so I might as well appease him and let him in. However, the last time I checked, he had the spare key. Please don't tell me he lost it. This is the third spare key —if he tells me he has lost it, I am going to glue the next one to his hand.

Stopping him before he makes further noise and alerts my entire apartment floor, I shout back a roar of my own. "Jack, if you don't have a hot black coffee with my name on it, I'm going to need you to turn around and not return until you have what I need to function."

No response, smart man.

Still drenched in sweat and looking the part of someone who obviously didn't get enough sleep, I begrudgingly make my way to my front door. I attempt to calm my heightened breaths and my thumping heart. Forever the workaholic bachelorette, it is safe to say my apartment edges on the side of messy. Not messy enough to have pests and rodents, although enough mess to declare that I'm married to my career.

The apartment isn't large by any means, but I don't make matters easier by covering every available surface with handwritten journals, piles of clothing, and medical textbooks. A small single-wide walkway is the only way to navigate between everything without knocking the piles off kilter. Each colorless wall from floor to ceiling is lined with bookshelves of various shapes and materials. Stacked so tightly it hardly leaves room for anything else.

My motherless adolescence was hell, so there aren't any happy smiling family portraits or heavily perfumed paraffin candles left out to fragrance the air when others come to visit. The piece of filth I call a father will never see the inside of this apartment, either in person or captured behind a lens. I impatiently wait for the day to come when I get the call announcing his death. A melodic symphony for my ears to be blessed with the location of his grave so I can spit my appreciation for him on his worthless carcass.

I don't entertain, I work long hours, read until late in the evening, and sleep. There are no knick-knacks scattered around, or personal touches to show my personality. Most nights are spent alone eating a pack of ramen noodles for dinner and catching up on the latest medical journal research.

Nothing sparks a relationship faster than, "Hi, I dissect dead people, nice to meet you." Oh, add in the fact that I never have enough time to complete laundry, and you'll soon understand why living in coveralls is a much easier option. The dead only tell the truth and aren't complicated. They leave no room for lies and deception. Their body tells me a story and it is my job to relay that story to find them justice and peace. If I am truly being honest with myself, I don't like people, so why bother attempting to date? The living are complicated and manipulative.

A boisterous whistling tune grinds through my ear canal the closer to the door I get, letting me know ahead of time the type of high energy I can expect from my closest friend and partner.

"Are you seriously whistling at this hour in the morning?" I proceed to shout, the closer my body carries me to my vibrant friend.

"Ray, it is 1:30 in the afternoon, what do you mean, at this hour in the morning?" he cheerfully retorts. His playful tone gives me reason to believe that I will find his usual Cheshire grin plastered ear to ear when I open this door.

"I only fell asleep a few hours ago. That is what I mean by this hour in the morning," I reply sarcastically.

Aggressively swinging the door open, I find none other than the most obnoxious morning person I've known in my entire life. Growing up as close friends and then going off to the same college, we have always been inseparable. Even though we are polar opposites in personality, I couldn't imagine a more supportive and grounding person to have in my life.

"Well don't you look happy to see me," he says joyously, holding two steaming cups of coffee.

"Look, Jack, you know the rule. You are not allowed to talk to me until I have had at least three sips of my coffee. Record timing though. I think that is the fastest you have ever made me want to punch you." His hand holding my coffee barely moves an inch in my direction, but I can instantly tell by the size of the cups which one is mine. Snatching my cup quickly, Jack doesn't have a second to blink before I leave him awkwardly standing in the front entrance to my apartment. He's been here more times that I can count. At this point, he is no longer a guest.

"Fine, *your majesty*, your devoted knight will be over here waiting while you shed your monster skin," he says, chuckling to himself while he indulges in his own cup.

After my required sips of liquid sustenance, I can feel the lurking shadows of my terror slowly fade back to their depths. The crushing weight previously squeezing into my shoulders begins to ease and release. I can survive under lack of sleep, it is the unmeasurable amount of fear and panic burning my body's fascial tissue that will cause me to explode outwardly. Each scalding hot gulp of Italian dark roast black sustenance chases away the aftermath of my stolen night's sleep. Caffeine no longer has any direct effects on my energetic state, my dependency level is a whole different story.

I've been keeping the intensity of my most recent spin of terrors hidden, cautiously avoiding the heart to heart speech Jack gives me every time these roll around. The only advice anyone ever seems to use as a solution is medicine and therapy. News flash... I have tried it all. No amount of talking to a therapist is going to help fend off the impending reality of night terrors. Not to mention, medicine makes me a zombie and leaves my brain feeling lost and confused. It severs the ties that allow me to access my full brain.

Peeking over his cup in my line of sight, Jack asks carefully, "Permission to speak?"

"Permission granted, but tread lightly," I reply, intentionally leaving an edgy tone in my voice.

"We got a ca—"

Colliding my fist down on the kitchen counter, my interruption slams the words back down his throat.

"Jack... Don't say it! Please don't say they found another

one." Grinding viciously, the audible scraping of my back molars can be heard over the tension-filled silence. I already knew what he was about to tell me, although I still held the tiniest sliver of hope he'd say something different.

"Another one... was found," he treads cautiously, bracing himself for my inevitable outburst.

"What do you mean they found another one?" I growl between gritted teeth.

"*Technically,* I said that another one was found, not that they found another one." Fury burns behind my piercing brown eyes, giving him every indication that I am not putting up with his shenanigans today. "Hikers came across the body last night and we're up."

"I don't want to deal with another one, Jack. Barely twelve hours ago, we were at the scene of the last victim. Crime scene number five, which means this morning's case is lucky number six and I'm not feeling so lucky. Dismemberment has already been checked off on this week's bingo card."

"I know you don't, but you know this case is a top priority that requires all hands on deck," he replies calmly.

I have no words left. None. Between the return of the most hated part of my mind and the relentless, bloodthirsty killer, my tank is empty. No amount of caffeine or prescribed magic blue pills can console my inner turmoil.

My thoughts become distant and incoherent. A detached look must have crept across my face, my stoney facade cracked and exposed. Jack continues to proceed using caution as he makes his way to stand next to me on my side of the kitchen island. These are the moments where he attempts to fix every broken part of me in a hug, instead, he pauses before making contact.

"They're back aren't they?" He inquires softly, concern etched on his face while also maintaining a safe distance.

I didn't have the heart to tell him yes, he already knew. The unmistakable dark circles, quick-to-anger attitude, and the ever-growing disdain for a job that never seems to destroy me. Until now. Aside from being coworkers for so many years, we have also been best friends for as long as I can count. He knows me better than myself. I don't have to explain the agony, fear, or visceral response that these terrors bring around each cycle. They affect not only me, but also my work efficiency, and my relationships involving everyone around me. Who wants to attempt to have a conversation with someone who hasn't slept in three days? I for one wouldn't, that's for damn sure.

"Earth to the zombie lady," he says, while slowly waving his hand entirely too close to my face, snapping me out of daunting thoughts. The tone edges on caution, then quickly reforms into his usual playful banter.

"Sorry, I zoned," I reply despondently, the lack of fight evident.

"Clearly. You sure you're okay to continue this case? How many days this time?"

"Currently going on six days and this pattern of terror isn't showing any sign of relinquishing its hold on me." There is no reason to lie, I just don't have the heart to tell him that I think I need a break. Rolling my head around in circles and inhaling a deep breath from my diaphragm, loud pops erupt in my joints, releasing built-up tension in my muscles.

I don't want to see the latest victim even though I know... I know that I can push it for at least one more. That is what I am supposed to say right? Push my sanity to the side so I can focus on finding yet another stain on society. That's what is most important. I knew what I signed up for when I decided to do this for a living.

Personal matters typically don't break through the work barrier I have placed, but something about this case has latched onto every fiber of my being and won't surrender its hold. Something about this unsub is proving to be difficult and unsettling, their motivation and drive unyielding. Their desire to release destruction and carnage at every scene exhibits their enjoyment and sadistic compulsion to brutalize each victim. Knowing what I know and seeing all that I have seen thus far, I am left with uncertainty that I will come out on the other side of this unscathed and without long-term effects.

Rather than Jack having time to interrogate me further, I scurry off to the bathroom to turn myself into someone who appears to be a functioning professional. Planting myself under the showerhead, I close my eyes and allow the scorching water to pound my body, leaving a small amount of hope that it will drown out images of the previous five victims. Their bodies were mutilated, cracked open, and displayed with no remorse, a hunter hanging his prized kill for everyone to witness. Eviscerated flesh and tissue showcased with no sign of respect for the deceased. No amount of soap is sufficient enough to wash their blood from my mind and body.

Saved once again by my friend and coworker, Jack's voice yanks me up from the downward spiral in my head. "Ray, hurry up, we have to get down there before they ruin the scene and darkness takes over. It's a bitch setting up the spotlights and you know it."

He doesn't have to wait long as he catches me stepping out of the bathroom dressed and ready to go. "Alright, let's get this day started then." I grab my work bag, a fresh set of coveralls, and start making my way toward the door.

"Just like that, you're ready to go?"

"Uh yeah," I retort, shoving my bag in his face.

"Lead the way then," he chuckles loudly, bending over at the waist with one arm folded over his abdomen and the other gesturing to the door.

Laughter is never in short supply when Jack is by my side.

2

THE SHORT TRIP DOWN THE WINDING MOUNTAIN ROADS TO CANADEE State Park is agonizingly quiet. Staring out the passenger window, vivid autumn colors blur past me, creating a mural of unique beauty around every hairpin turn. Warm rays from the sun penetrate through the windshield, leaving the inside of the car comfortable, and rendering the AC and heat useless. The constant stream of rock music typically found blasting out of the speakers in Jack's Toyota 4Runner doesn't play. No questions need to be asked. I know he's worried.

Glancing over at him periodically, I can see the concern etched on his face. His normal relaxed posture is replaced by an erect position and the tops of his knuckles whiten from the pressure of his grip on the steering wheel. Specks of blood begin to appear from him aggressively biting and gnawing at his bottom lip. He knows better than to open his mouth to share feelings, and I'm not the type that needs a pity party. I know whatever is going on will subside and life will hopefully see some reprieve soon enough.

What I am not sharing is that I can feel my anxiety increase the closer we get to our grim destination. An uncommon occurrence since I do what is not recommended —shove all of my doubts and worries to the bottomless depths of my psyche. Emotions are something I never fully understood and the time someone spends trying to understand them is something I consider useless. Thankfully, after a couple more turns, we will arrive at our destination and we can avoid this topic altogether, concentrating fully on our work. Stick to the case and then we can move on.

Stepping out of the vehicle, I halt temporarily to absorb one last ounce of calm reassurance before entering the whirlwind that lay ahead. Contrary to what my body's main frame is saying, I take a second for myself and remain thankful for the sunny yet crisp mid-autumn weather. Allergies no longer threaten to unravel me and I am left with the hope that maybe today won't be as bad as I know it can be. I want to give my senses a break rather than sending them straight to overdrive. A small blessing of clear air since the pungent scent of death will soon impale my nares.

Waiting to change into my coveralls, I stand comfortably by the side of the car, basking in one of my favorite times of year. Soft-locking my knees, I close my eyes and concentrate on what's happening around us. I hesitate mid-breath and open my eyes instantly. Noticing immediately in our surroundings, no birds are singing, no woodland creatures scavenging for the winter or scurrying in the trees, and no sounds of crinkling leaves. An unusually strange behavior out in nature, so my awareness switches to high alert. Silence is not what you come to expect and I can't help the alarm beginning to disturb my brief moment of peace. My pulse quickens and my head whips frantically around in search of answers. Flickering back to my night terror, the edge of panic creeps through me, and is suddenly chased away by Jack's presence once more.

"Hey Ray, you coming or what?" he asks, jerking his thumb and head in the direction of the crime scene.

"Yeah, be there in a sec, I thought I saw something. Let me put my shoes on and I'll be good to go," I call, hurrying to zip up my coveralls. Slipping my feet in my shoes, I grab the remaining parts of our gear from the trunk and take off in the direction Jack was heading. I know it isn't right to lie to him, we simply don't have time for my cracked stability right now.

It shouldn't take a genius to uncover why we are heading to this part of the trailhead. The attention this case has drummed up has put our town on the map. Most visitors drive straight through our small area when coming to experience their winter vacation in the mountains. The residents of Canadee pride themselves on remaining a close-knit town and not conforming to the pressures of big corporations coming in to build large resorts and casinos. Nothing like getting stranded by the snow in a cozy log cabin snuggled up in warm blankets by a blazing fire.

Easing our way between the rows of cars, I notice a rather large array of civilian vehicles. This can't be good. Everyone has shown up to catch a glimpse at the destruction our latest serial celebrity has accumulated. It will never cease to amaze me that for most people, this is still a game. A fabricated boogeyman to stir up excitement. No harm can come to them since they believe they are protected by their mental bubble, ignoring that this is a very real thing. I am repulsed by the actions this town has exhibited during the murders. No one ever believes it could happen to them or in their small town until it does and it is too late. Due to the ever-growing popularity of crime shows, most have begun a desensitization to all of the very real dangers that lurk behind dark corners. I firmly believe that if they saw every gruesome detail, they would not be so intrigued by the grotesque manner in which these victims died.

Navigating further along the unpaved rugged trail, the sounds of chitter-chatter and colliding voices thrum to life and echo throughout the forest path. An excited storm of pandemonium begins to fill my ears, sound now returning to this once silent place. Frantic comments are woven between the gawking eyes of spectators and the media outlets begging for answers. A frenzy of sharks circling their prey, hoping for that one story to make them big. Bright flashes from cameras and microphones are shoved urgently in our direction.

Is covering a serial killer story the only way to go? Is that honestly what people want to talk about? What happened to unbiased factual journalism?

Sergeant Miguel Hamlin, a long-time veteran of the Canadee police force stands firmly at the wooden barricades. A tall, burly mountain man exudes a booming voice who seems for the moment to have everything under control. Remaining focused on the crowd, he barely notices us when we approach him.

"What's up, Sarge?" Jack yells over the collision of voices.

Gesturing in the opposite direction, "The FNG, Levi, is with the vic. The biggest case we have ever had in our area and I can't believe they stuck me babysitting the fucking new guy. My ass will be the one on the chopping block if we don't catch this son of a bitch," Sgt. Hamlin huffs out, an apparent tone of annoyance and frustration rips backing each word.

Jack, being the unofficial mediator during tense moments, lands a firm hand on the shoulder of Sgt. Hamlin, "Don't fret, we've got your back." His optimistic inflection slices cleanly through any remaining trace of hesitancy and doubt.

"Good to know at least someone here does," the Sgt. scoffs.

As we attempt to walk discreetly away from the chaos, I do my best to try and ignore the shouts and questions bombarding us.

"What can you tell us about The Butcher of Canadee?" An overweight sleazeball journalist shouts in our direction.

I freeze mid-stride, crank my head, and glare in the direction the voice came from. Every last remaining ounce of patience I had formed a tight ball deep inside my chest cavity. A practiced refrain from punching this bastard's teeth down his throat.

"*The Who of What?*" I shout back, failing to hide any and all anger in my tone. "Innocent young women are dying and your only concern is information about the person responsible for this mayhem. What about the families? How do you think they feel? What if it was your loved one, would you want their death to be plastered across every media outlet and fantasized?"

Jack gently squeezes my shoulders and guides me away from their onslaught of questions and remarks. "Take a big breath and ignore them, Ray, they only want to get under your skin. Don't give them what they want."

"That's right, learn to follow directions and let a man be in charge," a cameraman speaks up from the crowd, a small circle forms around him so others can bear witness to his disrespect towards women.

"Better yet, I'm hungry, get back in the kitchen and make me a sandwich you useless bitch!" My previous abysmal encounter proceeds to croak out behind crooked, yellow-stained teeth. Only a few men are amused by the situation and chuckle quietly to themselves. One woman close by the action backhands the man laughing next to her and he stops instantly. A small victory.

I've trained my whole life to not put up with men's bullshit but always remained professional and dignified in my actions when under the scrutinizing eye of the public. Nothing is going to hold me back this time. I barrel over to the schmuck and double-fist his grease-stained collar. My 5 '11" frame towers over the pathetic excuse of a man. Mouth agape and breathing heavily, the repulsive stench of tooth decay and chronic halitosis singes my nose hairs. Shock with a hint of terror creeps across his face as he watches the seething rage pool in my dark brown eyes. *Inhale. Exhale.*

"You're not... Worth... My time," I spit out through gritted teeth and shove his repulsive body back into the crowd. Giving him no time for a rebuttal, I turn quickly on my heel and shout back in the direction of the reporter frenzy. "Someone call animal control, the mangy, rabid dogs were let out of their cages!"

Tolerating men similar to that scumbag started at a very young age for me. I might've only had sisters, but I had the up close and personal experience of surviving under the forceful fist of an alcoholic, piece of shit, incompetent father. From an outside perspective, it appeared that we had a comforting home life, contradicting the inside of our home where my dad wanted to drown us all in the bathtub and declare it an accident. No one batted an eye when my mother's mysterious death occurred, but those close enough to the family knew he got tired of beating her and threw her down the stairs instead. Their silence screamed loud enough for me to hear and understand that no one was coming to rescue us.

After so many years of abuse by him and sorry excuses labeled boyfriends, I refuse to allow men to think they have power over me just because I am a woman. Shaking my head to dissolve once painful memories, I remind myself of my current location, and how I no longer have time and energy for that vile excuse of a reporter. Nudging me in the arm, Jack and I resume our walk to the victim.

Stepping under the signature yellow caution tape barrier coiled around the trees, I prepare mentally for the death waiting for us around the corner.

3

THE GROWING UNSETTLING ENERGY OF MY NOW FAMILIAR DARK-
cloaked foe of shadows caresses up my spine once more.
Deeply coiling around the intricacies of my spinal column, a
sensation of death lingers behind each featherlike embrace.
Have I been here previously or am I reliving the nightmare
over and over again? *Keep it together. You can't do your job if
your mind is foggy, people depend on you.* My internal conflict
battles furiously to keep my mind focused and cognizant of
my surroundings.

The crunching of rocks and dead leaves ground my mind
and spirit the further we walk along the path. Uneven terrain
helps me zero in on the movement my body makes and rein-
forces stability. I notice a tall and slender woman in her mid-
forties, Officer Penelope Ren, standing off to the side, she

questions a couple dressed in hiking gear. Matching their clothes and their visible discomfort, logical reasoning leads me to believe these must be the two hikers who found our victim this morning. The middle-aged man makes a great effort to stand tall and composed, but his firm demeanor remains transparent when meeting his unblinking stare—a sign of shock. The woman next to him is visibly upset and beside herself. Inconsolable and paired with unmanageable tremors. Uncontrollable sobs pour from her mouth and eliminate any chance of coherent sentences. Good to know that someone around here is taking this matter seriously and isn't wrapped up in the glamorized versions of serial killers on TV.

Unlike the previous victims who were found much deeper in the center of the forest, we are closer to the hiking trail this time. Our unsub is spiraling, derailing, and losing the battle to remain organized and collected. Lacking a cooldown period between kills, I'm left to speculate that the killer is close by, watching the action unfold. Reveling in the attention he desperately craves. A sick disgrace that gets off on the suffering of others. The level of mutilation goes far beyond the typical parameters for piquerism and screams overkill. An unquenchable thirst for violence, destruction, and evisceration of his victims.

My final steps toward the victim's last moments on this Earth feel weighed down by cement. Familiar uneasiness screams across every synapse of my nervous system, my fight or flight response nears full amplification. The urge to close my eyes and retreat to the dark recesses of my mind calls to me. A metaphorical rope tightening its noose around my neck. Flying directly above me, a large black crow's screech clears the dark anguish clouding my mind. Blinking rapidly, the haziness lifts, and the comforting feeling of self-awareness returns in waves.

Standing on the outskirts of our perimeter looking lost and confused in his surroundings is a young man, roughly in his early twenties. Uniform appearing spotless and absent of any creases, this has to be the rookie the Sergeant wasn't pleased to have working today. A safe assumption that this is his first murder case. Fresh out of the academy and thrust into a gruesome serial killer investigation. No better way to break him in and get his feet wet. I'll be impressed if he has the stomach to stick around after this one, or if the ghostly pallor is a sign he will be heaving his lunch behind the tree adjacent to us.

Extending his right hand in front of the rookie, Jack drums up the best introduction voice he can muster. "You must be Levi, the FNG, I'm Jack and that's Rayna." He gestures in my direction.

Ignoring common courtesy, the rookie smacks Jack's hand out of the way and quips back, "You know, I'm getting real sick of that tag. Can someone tell me what the hell it means?"

"All in due time, rookie, all in due time," Jack makes little effort to smother the laugh behind the palm over his mouth.

"Can we get back to the reason why we have all been summoned here, please? Levi, what can you tell me about what happened here?" I inquire from the young rookie.

"Victim's name is Rebekah Musing, a 33-year-old female. According to her driver's license, she is 5'9 " and weighs 225 lbs. Found at 0900 hours by hikers on the trail. The woman found no pulse when she checked her carotid and was advised by the 9-1-1 operator to refrain from any life-saving efforts and to stay at the scene until we arrived. Her body was cool to the touch and showed no signs of life, so EMS ruled it DOA. They found her propped against the tree holding a boning knife in her right hand and an unknown object grasped in her left. Based on the first responders assessment, and the surroundings around the body, the sheriff is looking at ruling it a possible suicide and marking it unrelated to the string of murders."

"Care to explain the media storm then?" Jack questions.

"They're sharks and smelled blood in the water," Levi says and slowly retreats to stand away from the victim, his ashen hue becoming more apparent with each passing moment.

"Go sit down before you pass out and stay out of our way, we will take it from here," Jack spoke in a reassuring yet firm voice to the young kid.

"Sarge said I can't leave you guys unattended."

"Well, if you lose your lunch on our evidence, you can kiss that badge goodbye. Keep it together kid," I demand firmly, leaving little wiggle room for misunderstandings.

Last time I checked, it wasn't in my job description to console anyone, so I ignore the green—in color and rank—rookie, and get to work recording my on-site examination.

My initial reaction to the victim's body is unlike any I've had in all of my years as Chief Forensic Medical Examiner for the town of Canadee. Violent, gruesome, and grotesque crime scenes are endless in my profession, having new killers lining up to take the next vacant spot. Yet, in all of the sites I have been called to, all of the fatalities have been just that—tragic stories that needed to be told. If I sat back and allowed each victim's face and personal lives to worm their way into the forefront of my mind, I wouldn't be able to live. Sticking to the facts protects me from being consumed and over-whelmed by every human who ends up on my exam table. Never have I felt an instant attachment, until now.

My feet stop immediately, frozen in place, a sharp inhale of breath escapes my lips. An overwhelming flood of emotions burst inside my chest, weakening me at my knees. My strength and willpower are all I have and within a fraction of a second, pulled out from underneath my feet as if I never held it in my grasp at all.

Propped against a thick red maple tree, Rebekah sits motionless. Fallen leaves of rich golds, vibrant oranges, and claret lay cascaded around her, as if a single leaf dared not to touch her. Shades of natural auburn hair lay delicately around her face, blending seamlessly with the autumn leaves. The forest appears to have mourned the loss of this beautifully magical spirit.

Despite the waterfalls of coagulated blood that cover her stunning frame, I am most gobsmacked by the expression on her face. A deep sense of peace paints her features, unmarred serenity and untouched by the dark evils of this world and the next. Looking beyond the shades of death, the natural pink undertone of her porcelain skin shines through, a near match to my own. Even behind closed eyelids, I can feel her gaze locked on mine, a story yet to be told and one that will shock us all. Deep, burnt, crimson blood, dried and cracked, covers the gaping wound on her arm and surrounding tissue. Foreign debris is scattered intermittently in the exposed tissue from the falling leaves and wind with the sharp smell of iron present in the air.

4

AN UNEXPLAINED, REFINED RESTRAINT WAS SHOWN IN THIS KILL. This unsub's previous victims displayed the sick, sadistic pleasure each death brought. Whoever is killing these women, their violence increases with each murder, and their bloodlust craves more destruction. The question of why the sixth victim's kill is different bounces around unanswered in my head. Victimology is almost spot-on for each woman, so what is the driving force behind these merciless kills?

"Tell me your story and I promise it will be shared to protect others," I whisper to myself before grabbing my recorder and beginning my assessment.

"Preliminary examination of Rebekah Musing. Victim presents with a vertical laceration extending from the palmar surface of her left hand upward through her carpus to the cubital

fossa. Pronounced severing of the pronator teres, flexor carpi radi-
alis, palmaris longus, flexor carpi ulnaris, and the flexor digi-
torum superficialis. Adipose and fascial tissue structures protrude
externally along the wound. Exposure of the ulna is also present.
Laceration appears to be performed in a distal to proximal direc-
tion. No hesitancy in the cut. Significant blood loss due to the
location of the wound.

At this time, the anterior interosseous artery, the ulnar artery,
and the brachial artery appear to be severed. The person or
persons responsible had anatomical knowledge and knew where
the cut would be most efficient. Scattered ecchymosis in various
stages of healing is present on the victim's arms and legs. Signifi-
cant deep purple discoloration is visible across the lower iliac
region and migrating up into the umbilical area, displaying
evidence of broken blood vessels pooling under the skin. Possible
blunt force trauma to that area. Internal hemorrhaging is
suspected. Jagged, hyperpigmented, and raised scar tissue appears
bi-laterally on the lower legs and posterior trunk. Further tissue
examination will be required to provide a full list of injuries,
internal and external. Peak rigor mortis is exhibited. Estimated
time of death around 0100 hours."

Levi clenches his hand over his mouth and pinches his
nose prior to speaking to Jack. "Did you understand a word
she just said?" He aims to whisper, except his voice squeaks
out in a whistle tone.

"First off, you're being childish and disrespectful, remove
your hands from your face and toughen up. To answer your
question, you'd be surprised to find that yes, I do understand
her. It also helps that we went to the same college, took the
same classes, and passed the same boards. We are both
medical examiners with additional training in forensic
pathology and law enforcement procedures. Dr. Rayna Pierce
is brilliant in this field and will remain at the top for the fore-

seeable future," Jack replies, anger seeping venomously into each word he directs toward the nauseated rookie.

"So uh, care to enlighten me then?" Levi continues to question, a hint of annoyance and ridicule forming in his words. A demonstration of his lack of respect for authority.

Jack stands up from his crouched position and lines up toe to toe with the rookie. "Let me put this to you in terms that an incompetent kid like yourself will understand. The victim... Sliced... Her arm... Badly, and now she doesn't breathe."

"Well, no fucking shit, Sherlock. It seriously takes all those words to say, *'She sliced her arm badly and died?'*" Levi says, dumbing his voice in a mocking tone towards Jack's childlike description.

"If she wanted someone holding the education level of a squirrel to understand, she would have dumbed it down to your level," Jack quips, adding an arch to his brow.

"Oh, fuck you! I am way smarter than a squir—" Suddenly, an acorn falls from a tree above their heads, hitting Levi, and interrupting his rant. A chittering almost like laughter, rings out from the branches above, and a bushy tail can be seen disappearing into a cluster of branches.

"HA! See, even the damn squirrel is offended, you prick!" Jack laughs, clutching his side.

"Jack! Levi! When you're done comparing the size of your genitalia, document photos of her left hand, I need to examine underneath it."

"Sir, yes sir, boss ma'am. Let me hop right on that for you," Jack sarcastically answers, never taking his eyes off of Levi.

"Jack Nicholas Miller! Now!"

A quick turn of his head and a spin on his heels, Jack is at my side again.

Now that the grown children have been successfully reined in, we can get back on task. Kneeling back down to continue to process the scene, I hesitate before delicately reaching for the medallion. Enigmatic forces ensnare me in a web of mystery, leaving nothing in my arsenal of historical knowledge that can explain where it came from or what time period. Small amounts of gold filigree untouched by her death stand out between each of her curved fingers. The remaining details are lost underneath layers of dried blood and dirt.

Anticipation roars through me at the thought of finding something that will give us any indication as to what we are up against. Mere seconds after Jack captures the required evidence, my desire for answers takes over and I can get to work freeing the mystery. It's a slow process of uncurling her cold, rigid fingers from around the object. The coagulated blood in her palm has acted similar to a vacuum, suctioning the medallion to her skin. Using precise focus and concentrated effort, the unique gold medallion lifts freely from her grasp.

At first glance, I notice no distinct identifying markers, no indication of time period, and much to my dismay, no answers to lead us to the killer. I am no stranger to research, so finding out where the medallion came from will be a task that I refuse to back down from. However, there is one thing I can form an educated guess about and that is the fact that this artifact is an antique and made of pure gold due to its weight.

Beneath some of the blood, grime, and dirt, I can make out the shape of a large, polished, garnet gem resting in the center. Surrounding the center jewel, a circle of gold skulls set in elaborate leaf filigree finishes the next layer, creating depth within one piece. Protruding from underneath the skulls are eight arrows of identical size pointing outward. Engulfed by this secret, my surroundings fade around me and for a moment, I forget where I am. This perplexing force amplified tenfold once freed and held in my hands.

Earth to Rayna, snap out of it, I scold myself.

Pressing firmly into the dried blood in an attempt to clean the object, the arrow-shaped spikes stab outward, slicing through my gloves and into my skin. Vibrant red blood bursts from the horizontal lacerations on my middle three digits and anterior palm. Digital arterial squirts all over my fresh set of navy blue coveralls, painting me in splatters and abstract lines of crimson.

"FUCK!" I exclaim, jerking my right hand away swiftly, unprofessionally dropping the medallion immediately. I dart backward in fear of contaminating the crime scene. Witnessing the event, Jack races to my side.

"Ray, are you okay? What happened?" Jack asks in a panic, inspecting my now blood-soaked hand.

"Levi, get E—," the words hadn't fully left my mouth when Levi's lanky frame plummets to the ground, fainting at the first squirt of fresh blood.

"Annnd, he's out of here!" Jack mocks, while making an effort to help me stop the gushing blood forming in my palm.

"Enough! I'm fine. Go finish working," I scold, making sure irritation and disapproval is connected to my words.

"Okay, okay, don't expect me to pick you up when you fall over from blood loss," Jack replies jokingly, leaving me standing by myself again.

Within minutes, emergency personnel are at my side assessing my new injuries. An older woman, roughly in her late sixties, springs into action and reaches for my injured hand. "Ma'am, please sit down and let me take a look. You've lost a significant amount of blood already."

"I am ignoring the fact that you just called me ma'am. I'm fine. Please clean the wound and let me get back to why I am here in the first place," I reply sharply, eyes cutting to the defenseless responder.

Treading carefully and casting her gaze downward, she resumes her attempt to follow procedure. Their protocols mean little to me when I have an unsolved serial killer case sitting directly in front of me. I observe as she takes a deep inhale and exhales before continuing, exuding a calm, calculated tone.

"Dr. Pierce, please consent to me cleaning the wound and suture your injuries before allowing your return to the scene."

"Fine. I'm consenting to sutures, a standard blood panel, and a chem 7, nothing more," I reply sternly, frustration evident in my tone.

I am not ignorant to the fact that I need sutures, I sliced the arteries and continue to lose more blood with each pump of my heart. But I desire to return to finish my work.

A fresh imprint of my teeth from holding my tongue and roughly fifteen silently agonizing minutes later, my right hand is covered in bandages and I am free to resume my duties. One step out of the ambulance and I am stopped by Jack. *What now?*

"How're you feeling? You lost a lot of blood and made me worried."

I glance back at the older EMT before responding to my overprotective friend. "I'm okay, I can handle sutures, I just want to get back to my examination."

"Um, I know you're going to be mad, but the techs and I finished, boss. We are preparing to head back to the lab now," Jack replies, slowly taking a step back and preparing for my argumentative rebuttal.

Encountering his timidness around me, you would think I hit him constantly or scream endlessly but that isn't the case, he is perpetually afraid of being the bearer of bad news. Stemming from our rough upbringings, he understands my short temper and needs to lash out irrationally

"Fine, let's go."

Jack eyes me quizzically, accompanied by a high arch in his brows, responds cautiously, "That's it? No argument?"

"Jack, you have pushed my boundaries too far today and I am at my limit. I know how much you care. Sometimes—" I cut off my own words instead of making the situation worse, plus I don't appreciate having EMS as an audience. Without divulging any weakness, I skim over the surface of my bodily assessment, only because he is my friend and will dig at me until I tell him. "My hand throbs and the skull-crushing pain that I felt this afternoon has yet to relent. Let's get back to the lab, perform the autopsy, and catch this son of a bitch."

Unknown

"Come to me, my Queen, I have been waiting a long time for you."

5

A LOOK CAN SAY A THOUSAND WORDS, SO WHEN I HOLD MY HAND out for Jack's keys, the pause before handing them over is damn near undetectable, a battle of power that he won't win. Experiencing this amount of blood loss and the severe lack of sleep tearing inside my body is a terrible combination to place behind the wheel of a vehicle.

We both know I need these few moments of solitude before returning to the chaos. He won't defeat me in an evidence-based debate right now, so I am pushing the friendship bond to the edge.

After so many years of being independent in all aspects of life, it is easy to forget that it's okay to rely on those around you. I simply refuse to have someone dictate what I do to my own body. Discipline growing up was harsh and instilled that no one is going to save you, and finding safety and comfort from others is damn near impossible. Somehow, life knew I needed someone like Jack to keep my head above water. But in this moment, I'd prefer to drown.

Arriving back at the morgue, I long for nothing more than to sit back and close my eyes. The weight of my eyelids increases with each blink, my dry tear ducts begging for relief. Unfortunately, that isn't a possibility considering the current fractured state of my brain. Plus, Jack and the technicians will be arriving momentarily, so I don't have excess amounts of time to myself. I understand the correct course of action is to complete the autopsy, report my findings, and then take care of myself, but this has to be the hardest I have pushed my body, so consequences are piling up. My body pushes catastrophic levels of weakness. Besides coffee and energy drinks, I don't believe I've eaten more than an orange in the last forty-eight hours.

Vice grip pressure threatens to fracture my skull from the inside out, distorting my vision as well. Daytime exacerbates the dysfunction and when I'm supposed to be healing during sleep, I am kept awake by a faceless entity stalking me like prey in the woods. I am not seeing a metaphorical light at the end of this tunnel, only darkness and despair.

I sit down at my desk intending to chart the preliminary assessment, although that is proving difficult, my own voice recording sounds foreign and incomprehensible. The blinking cursor mocks me as it hovers over the negligence of a blank chart. The victim... no, Rebekah needs this. She needs me to figure out the answers and fill in all of the missing puzzle pieces. I am convinced she is the missing link to this case, we have yet to figure it out. The other victims and their families deserve this as well.

For the first time in my life, I feel incompetent. The

weight of my responsibilities crashes over me and over-whelms every system in my body. Searching for a small minute of my peace, I surrender to my exhaustion, succumbing to the pressure of the world around me, and rest my head atop my desk. The sensation that came over me in the woods today told me everything I needed to know about how my evening was going to go, but I couldn't hold off any longer. My unwelcome foe is waiting for me.

Unknown

Two Days Ago

IT IS NO SECRET I HAVE A TYPE, A DISTINCT MOTIVATION, AND A *predictable profile. This fear keeps them up late at night, tossing and turning, finding no solace in their dreams. Death calls to them, a fly dangerously drawn to the chaos of a spider's web. Closely resembling, but none as deliciously enticing and powerful as my scarlet Queen. Kyla James will have to be another pawn on my quest for her. A prized victory displayed for her viewing plea-sure and the correct dosage for her to visit me once more.*

Running... Again. She knows that she can't outrun me and yet she tries anyway. Reeking of fear and desperation, she is foolish and loses all sense of knowledge and prior training. Flight tram-pling over any remaining trace of fight left in her body. If only I could convince her I desired to have a nice chat. A one-sided conversation with the sharp end of my knife, her screams and bellows a delicious appetizing symphony for my ears to feast upon.

Kyla might not have been able to see me coming, but somewhere deep behind the walls of her mind, she must have known she was going to be chosen. Her and the other useless pawns were cheap imitations of my Queen, the one true masterpiece. My prey is dumb enough to choose the same path as the others. The woods, they always choose the woods. Stupid girl. This dark wasteland is my playground, a field where I have the advantage and my ruthless nature can flood to the surface. No wandering eyes to interrupt my ascend to power and consumption.

Blended watercolors of dusk paint the sky, and among the thick tree trunks and fall foliage, the darkness of twilight blankets the woods, providing light to only those familiar with the shadows. Her echoing faint cries of discomfort and a classic vibrant trail of splattered blood shows me every directional change and hesitation my beautiful catch makes. A minor injury acquired while foolishly running away from me. I want to stop and savor each drop on my tongue, but stalking after my prize is too enticing to miss. Her attempts to evade me prove to be useless and a waste of her energy. I could have caught her already, but I enjoy taking my time.

I savor the scent of fear and the undeniable sound of her heart pounding relentlessly against her constricting ribcage.

She fails miserably in controlling her deep gulps for air while looking back every few steps with hope of vanishing from her faceless monster. The enemy lurking in the shadows, watching and waiting to unleash the unavoidable destruction planned out for her body. Thriving in the darkness gives me the perfect view of the beads of sweat covering her forehead and the redness developing on her cheeks.

She is going to taste so delicious.

The unmistakable sound of a branch cracking directly in front of me sends a wicked jolt of desire from my head to my toes. Following the snap, a scream dipped in pure desperation and anguish reverberates off the trees and directly to my ears. I'm so close now, my mouth salivating uncontrollably and my own heart screaming in anticipation. The predator always wins.

Scurrying back in a futile attempt to escape me, my prey speaks. "Pl-please don't h-hurt me. Please." Digging her fingers into the dirt behind her, more failed efforts send her further into panic. Sobs escape her quivering lips, mascara coating her cheeks in black streaks. The visibility of her frantic pulse screams under her flesh, captivating my vision momentarily. A wicked grin paints my own face ear to ear, "Oh, my sweet, you have got to do better than that."

"I haven't done anything wrong, why are you doing this? You don't have to do this."

"Your begging is pathetic and proves exactly why you were chosen." My face grimaces in disgust as her sobs continue to escape her pitiful mouth. Her deplorable begging will not destroy this for me.

"Ch-chosen for what?"

"You are going to feed me. More specifically, I have chosen your heart. Your spirit and your life force is now mine to consume. To revel in your essence coating my tongue and throat."

Realization dawns on her face at the severity of her situation. Her shock encompasses her mind and blocks out what sent her crashing to the forest floor.

My eyes gravitate to the seeping wound on her lower leg, the mouthwatering appearance of bone piercing through the skin. The metallic scent alone flares my nostrils and sends my head into a frenzy. I stalk closer, my tall imposing frame standing overtop of her. Closing the distance between us, I finally allow her to see the face hell-bent on annihilating her. Astonishment and disbelief distorts her makeup-stained face. She is unprepared for her killer.

Her voice croaks out faintly, "Rr-Rebakah? Is th-that you? How can you do this?"

"Her flesh is just a suit for me to use temporarily, a near-perfect, delectable host. Your friend has no control here, incapacitated and caged in her own mind."

Kyla remains frozen in shock by my words and actions, so I bask in her paralyzed state and lurk closer to her petite frame. She is a lot smaller than what I usually choose, but beggars can't be choosers when demanding a certain caliber meal. Intentionally glancing upward from the lower half of her body to capture her attention, I take my time dragging my tongue from her wrenched ankle to her black and purple discolored knee. Warm lifeblood and severed muscle fibers fill my mouth, staining my teeth a delightful shade of crimson.

Carnal desire for flesh and sinew excites me. Her blood mixed with salty sweat tastes divine and I don't miss my opportunity to sink deeper between the gaping flesh of the wound, drawing out more guttural screams of pain from my actions.

"Yes, scream for me. Feed me your pain."

Once I've had my momentary fill of her blood and feasting on her exquisite screams meant only for me, it is time for my favorite part of the evening... destroying every last ounce of her mind, body, and spirit.

Aggressively snatching her by her ankles, I remove the chain dangling from my neck and start my preferred process of displaying my prey upside down for all to see. Squeezing her lower legs together brings forth more screams of agony, edging exquisitely toward her loss of consciousness. Her head bobbles backward as the suffering becomes unbearable. My choice of chains allows for little movement and my sweet meal can't easily slip out of them. Contorting and writhing under the link's pressure mangles, and tears the skin savagely, eliciting irresistible colors of black and purple.

Dangling from one end of my chain is a freshly sharpened, two-way, stainless steel butcher's hook. Prolonging my own gratification, my tongue juts out of my mouth and coats the hooks in red-tinted saliva. Electricity courses through my body knowing one of my favorite parts is soon to unfold, an orgasmic climax set to explode. My eyes dart back to my prey's ankles right before I quickly pierce each sharp end into flesh, slicing cleanly through the lower leg muscles and the Achilles. A steady flow of fresh blood pours heavily down her porcelain skin. I want to bathe in her bloody blanket of warmth.

Shock from her previous injury keeps her deeply hidden behind a wall of darkness. I use this opportunity to throw the remaining chain around the thick tree limb and hoist her unconscious body upward. This change of position instantly jolts my prey awake, a fresh release of adrenaline now pulsing in her veins.

"Welcome back, my sweet. I love it when my prey is awake to feel me kill them."

She tugs immediately using her hands and feet, the reality of her situation takes a firmer hold, her voice distorts and quivers under the position, a deep bellow escaping her, "PLEASE DON'T DO THIS! PLEASE, LET ME GO!"

"What did I say about begging?! You are mine now and that is not changing. Remove those thoughts from that brain of yours and accept your fate."

Her body flails around in failed efforts of escaping and her feral screams set my skin ablaze with perfect precision.

"Any last words?"

"I lov—"

"Time is up!"

I impale my sharp blade into her belly button and slash the carving knife downward through her abdomen, decimating her torso. Instantly, I am bathed in hot, viscous arterial spray. Her fileted abdomen split magnificently, sending her intestines cascading into my lap and a geyser of blood continuously coating me as well as her dangling form. Punctured lungs squeeze and flutter, gasping for life, but only manage to choke and drown in heavy amounts of blood. I watch intently as the last remaining ticks and jolts shudder until there is no life remaining and the once steady beat removes this creature from this world.

Reveling in the euphoric nature of my kill, I move my hands to the smaller muscles of the ribcage, my sharpened knife being insufficient to go cleanly through the breastbone. The most satisfying part is taking my bare hands, ripping open the chest, and splitting the ribs utilizing my own strength. Squelching sounds of tearing muscles ring orgasmically through my ears, sending tantalizing sensations up and down my spine. Cracking under the pressure, they separate immediately, revealing an engorged crimson-painted masterpiece. Delicately carving around the once-beating heart, I remove the delicacy from the protective sac.

No longer beating and warm to the touch, its call to me doesn't cease. A merciless craving, an insatiable quench for dominance and power. Saliva saturates my tongue and cheeks, dripping from my mouth in unbridled anticipation. My top lip curls back to expose the sharpened points of my teeth. There is no other bite quite like the first one—an exquisite otherworldly experience unlike any other. Piercing effortlessly through my meal, warm lifeblood pours freely into my mouth, trails down the corner of my lips, and trickles across my chin, eliciting soft moans of satiation. With each bite, the feeling of strength, power, and control continues to forge fibrously together, momentarily creating a more corporeal form.

Finishing the last remaining remnants of my kill, I sit back and admire the handiwork of my fifth cuisine, each one tastier and more satisfying than the last, but never enough to make me whole. Displayed proudly for all eyes to see, I slither my way back to the shadows and wait for my Queen to visit me in her hours of rest.

The anticipation of her arrival sends a fresh array of sensations through my body.

6

"RAYNA! WAKE UP!" JACK SHOUTS.

His strong arms reach under my biceps gently and purposefully pulling me from my desk chair, securing me in his lap on the floor. I gasp repeatedly, inhaling the biggest gulps of air I can force into my lungs. Instantly becoming nauseous from the jolting position, my throat closes off to swallow acid back down my esophagus. Finding it difficult to form words, I just stare up at him blankly while he holds me close to him.

For the first time, I become aware of the solace in his embrace, his touch soothing rather than overstimulating. Tears waterfall down my cheeks, silently sobbing. Jack rocks me carefully against his chest, whispering softly in my ear,

"It's okay, it's okay, you're safe now. Deep breaths." His tone layered in fear and his expression coated in panic.

"I-I... I saw her." The words croak out from behind cracked, dry lips. My throat, hoarse and swollen, a faint metallic taste lingering on the back of my tongue. I must have crushed the muscle until my teeth pierced through flesh during this round of terror. Sensations of glass splitting my esophagus burn as I swallow. Every fiber of connective tissue remains locked and guarded despite my heart rate slowly returning to normal.

Jack moves his hands from around my waist to caress the left side of my face, an action woven with gentility and affection he has never shown to me before. "Who? Who did you see? Tell me Ray, it will all be okay. I've got you." Calm reassurance hangs in the air following his plea.

Using my fragile state to his advantage, he moves his fingers from the side of my face and strokes my wavy, sweat-soaked hair. His actions mimic those of someone consoling a loved one, another foreign act of compassion directed at me. Touch scares me, however, at this moment, my body yearns for it. The steady rhythm of his heart beats heavily under my ear, a soothing metronome of comfort. In my relaxing haze, I almost missed the hint of earthy cologne that lingers under his sweat entwined in his natural aroma.

The words are on the tip of my tongue, although I am having so much difficulty forming sentences to tell Jack the horror that I just experienced. I'm in utter disbelief. Rebekah had a story to tell me, and I was blind to the severity of her tale. What snapped in her mind to allow her to become so violent and cannibalistic?

Regaining some composure, I remove myself from Jack's embrace and make my way to the small couch a few feet away from my office desk. I'm unsteady on my legs, but I do my best to hide this lack of bodily control. Not only am I struggling to explain my side of the story, I'm now left with a lingering suspicion about the clarity of Jack's mind. A well-established boundary has always been in place between the two of us and he just tore cleanly through without thinking, myself included. Why am I focused on how I feel in his arms and how all-consuming his scent is to me? My lack of sleep continues to play games with my life and I want no part of it. Relationships don't work for me.

Closing my eyes to refocus on taking slow and calculated breaths, I strive to form sentences from the words balled in the back of my throat. "Rebekah is the murderer."

Jack's thoughts remain unheard as he removes himself from where we sat on the cold floor. Bracing his right palm against the wall for stability, his body language hardens before entertaining what I suggested.

"How do—" The sentence ends before he can finish his thought. Puzzlement of what I am suggesting eats away at his facial features. Relaxed brows now form deep furrowed lines across his forehead and right above the bridge of his nose. Uplifted corners of his mouth showing matching smile lines are no longer evident and replaced with closed lips in a tight line. The masseter muscles of his jaw flex and relax simultaneously with the temporalis muscles above his ear.

Never before have I witnessed Jack clench his teeth so firmly and exhibit such unexpected behavior.

Sitting on the edge of the couch, my elbows resting on my knees, I lean forward in defeat. Lightly cradling my throbbing head in my injured hand, I avoid his fixed gaze on me. Usually, I am the skeptical one, but Jack isn't even close to entertaining this outlandish story. I can't blame him. However, I am the one pushing this narrative, he has no other choice other than to believe me. Why would I waste time making up an elaborate story when we have so many people counting on us?

Unable to handle the silence any longer, I lean back against the couch and raise my arms in defense before speaking. "Hold on, let me explain first." I keep the tone in my voice calm and neutral to ease his frustration and perplexed nature in anticipation of him tuning out what I have to say. "I don't know how, but my nightmares are linked to this case. It wasn't until last night's terror and the location of Rebekah's body today that I was able to make the connection."

"Ray, you've seen her body. Even factoring in her height and musculature, I find it hard to believe she was the one to string those girls from a tree and disembowel them." Hardened doubt remains in his tone.

Coming from me, I know this is far-fetched, but he has to hear how genuine my words are. If I can't get my best friend to comprehend some of this, I run the risk of losing everything I've worked for in my life.

"You just woke me up from experiencing a first-hand perspective of her killing victim number five, Kyla James. I was trapped in Rebekah's mind, somehow witnessing the devastation from start to finish." I hesitate continuing to allow time for Jack's mind to regain composure. His shoulders descend slowly and his facial features soften with each heavy exhale—a sign he is returning to his normal demeanor. A soft hold of my breath occurs in anticipation of what words he will speak next.

"That might explain why she killed herself not long after killing Kyla. Are we positive she killed all of the victims?"

My ears perk up at his unforeseen acceptance. "I only witnessed Kyla's. The other murders are too similar in profile and victimology for them to be performed by multiple people. The experience is rather perplexing and I am struggling to comprehend the nature of the nightmare. There is no scientific evidence I can share to further prove myself."

For the first time in a long time, failure washes over me, my sutured hand being the only thing preventing me from smashing my face into the coffee table.

Jack walks over to where I sit on our office couch, wraps his arms around me for the second time today, and pulls me closer to him. "Why don't you start from the beginning and I will try to remain quiet until you're done explaining everything."

I ignore his close proximity and ground myself. Focusing on the facts of my terrors instead of the visceral turmoil they cause, I mentally prepare to recall my most recent encounter.

"After I got back to the morgue, I couldn't hold back the exhaustion any longer and my head rested on my desk faster than I could hold off. Immediately, I was thrust into Rebekah chasing Kyla through the woods, but I was just a passenger along for a ride through the eyes of our murderer. Her body thrummed with vibrations of satisfaction as she stalked Kyla through the woods, and I could feel the enjoyment grow the farther she walked. There was a craving in each passing moment and the closer she caught up to Kyla, the desire for carnage consumed each thought. It was as if..." My words trailed off, my sentence left unfinished.

Noticing my prolonged pause and unending thought, Jack squeezes my non-sutured hand to get my attention, bringing me back to reality.

"Sorry, something about this is rather unnerving and more complex of a puzzle than I imagined it to be. Rebekah might have been wearing different clothing and shoes, but I know it was her. So how do I justify this as expert analysis? I could hear her—Wait!" Jerking my body to attention, Jack stiffens abruptly at my side and prepares for action. "The thoughts I was hearing weren't hers."

"I'm sorry, what? I am not picking up what you're putting down. You have officially lost me." A soft chuckle follows, indicating he is now going to fully humor me in this wicked fantasy he believes I have drummed up.

Facing each other now, I am determined for him to listen to me. "It's crazy, I know. Try to stay with me. I just told you that I was a passenger along for a ride, right? Well, I was also experiencing the emotions and sensations happening within her system. As the gap between her and Kyla diminished, her body felt more foreign and the remaining tatters of her thoughts weakened, only to be replaced by a darker, more sinister tone."

"Okay, let me get this straight," he says firmly, adding a definitive pause at the end.

Up until now, he has only shown concern for my mental capacity and hasn't directed his focus to the events that are causing me such distress. With a fading pause, he continues his questions, the wheel fiercely turning in his mind.

Using his hands to further accentuate his point, he continues, "You want me to believe that while you slept, you projected back in time somehow and into a serial killer's mind at the exact moment they were annihilating a victim?"

"As someone who uses facts and statistical analysis to justify everything, I understand that none of what I am saying is making sense, but you have to believe me. I was there. I felt everything. I can still hear the growling undertone of a man's distorted voice when he spoke to Kyla. His thoughts held the same tonal inflection."

"I am not doubting you, I am just trying to wrap my head around the idea that you witnessed a murder from inside the mind of the killer," he pauses. "You also never finished your thought. What happened after you noticed the voice distorting?"

Knowing this was the worst part of my afternoon terror, I proceeded forward with caution. Sensing my hesitancy, Jack broke our agreement once more and reached over to place a reassuring hand on my leg, just above my knee. Emotional stability internally split immediately. I am thoroughly confused by his actions, while also finding strength in such a simple gesture.

"Once Rebekah's body caught up to Kyla, the voice changed significantly and the actions mimicked those of someone experiencing acute psychosis. The killer feasted on Kyla's blood, relishing in the pain they were causing with their mental and physical torment. Spoken words projected incoherently, except the anguish and terror contorting her facial features were indisputable. Helpless and bound in a spectating state, I was forced to watch the chained binding and mutilation of an innocent young woman. Each of the first five victims suffered immensely before taking their last breath. Something about victim number five was different in some way. I was shown this kill for a sick, demented purpose, but am unable to come up with a logical reason for it."

"I'm sorry Ray, I genuinely am." Even in the apology, I can hear the curiosity in his tone and desire to ask the final question, one that I don't want to relive.

"I hate to ask this, but did you find out what is happening to their hearts?"

"If Rebekah's body is the host killer of all five victims, then the noncorporeal, parasitic killer is forcing her to eat them."

Recoiling his hand away from my leg, Jack's face pauses in disbelief. "You're joking. Please tell me you're kidding."

7

TWO WEEKS AGO

ONE MONTH... THAT'S HOW LONG IT HAS BEEN SINCE I BURIED MY grandmother. Thirty long and agonizing days since I said a final goodbye to the most beautiful soul and kind-hearted woman I have ever had the pleasure of knowing. A woman who didn't contemplate the quick decision and took me in as a young child after discovering my mother was brutally murdered. One month of living back in the home I grew up in, wandering the same creaky hallways staring at the photo-clad, plaster walls that held onto the memories of the happiest times in my life. It used to be just her and I, no need, or room for anyone else.

My useless father abandoned my mother when she found out about the pregnancy and my grandfather was spending his life behind bars for crimes I knew nothing about. That was all I was told. Nothing more, nothing less. Not once, in my entire life, had she gone to see him or held conversations with me about him. As wonderful as my grandmother was, there were some things she held very close to her chest and consistently avoided answering any of my questions. As I got older, I became bolder and pushed harder for answers, but her demand for secrecy outweighed exposing the truth I so desperately longed for.

My grandmother lives, or should I say that I live, and am a returning resident to this old Dutch Colonial home built in the late 1920's. Sequestered at the end of Sycamore Street and nestled between the arms of the surrounding trees, it once stood to be the most beautiful house on the block. Lush green gardens covered in vibrant flowers and bright foliage used to amplify the craftsmanship of this divine structure. Stunning red maple trees enveloping the property bloomed striking branches filled with a blend of captivating foliage. Now, it appears to be an uninhabitable, abandoned house due for demolition. A large white house displaying peeling, cracked paint, broken gray shutters that hang precariously loose, wobbly red brick front steps, and a wrap-around porch reaching to one of the back doors with broken wooden steps leading to the back yard. Thick, dense vines protrude from the ground below, consuming large sections of the side of the house and extending upwards around the exposed brick chimney. My favorite afternoon reading spot nestled under the largest red maple tree is now littered with fallen branches, debris, and rough stones. The warm touch of life, no longer inviting and welcome.

Since my grandmother's death, I have slowly begun to reintroduce myself to these familiar walls. Embrace what once felt like soothing inviting hugs around every corner and remove the echoing hollow void. The task of cleaning and restoring this magnificent home to some of its former glory is daunting, but I find solace in the late hours of the evening when the last few rays of the sun linger in the window. Spanning four levels, including the sealed basement and the attic, I've chosen a different level each week to focus on cleaning and dumping the massive piles of junk my grandmother always refused to throw away.

This week's tough project is the attic, the one area of this grandiose home that I was not allowed to be in. Unbeknownst to my grandmother, this floor is the one place that perplexed me the most. There has always been an unsettling energy emitting from this part of the house. A push and pull that dared me to enter its hidden realm locked away tightly upstairs, a haunting whisper, a sweet call of exploration.

Covered in rust and old build-up of dirt, it takes a few tries of wiggling the skeleton key back and forth, combined with shoving my weight forcefully against the door for it to budge. Plumes of dust particles come careening out of the door, billowing around me in all directions. Holding my breath to avoid the impact of musk doesn't help because ingesting a cloud of stale air mixed with dirt and grime sends my lungs into a gasping fit. Bracing my arms against the wooden frame of the attic door, relentless coughing immobilizes me temporarily. After what feels like endless minutes of seizing, I can catch my breath and allow my eyes to settle on what lay before me in the attic.

I expected the floor-to-ceiling to be covered with boxes, old furniture, and useless nonsense that had no reason staying locked away. What shocks me most is how organized the attic remains. The exposed raw wooden beams to the left remain clean of clutter and to my right are six neatly stacked cardboard boxes labeled photos. My brows furrow deeply, drawing the left eyebrow higher than the other. Looking around I notice that even though every surface is covered in thick layers of dust, cobwebs, and filth, this room remains the most preserved. Frozen, unfinished in a capsule of time when my grandmother would utilize this space.

Resting under a small circular window centered on the back wall, I catch sight of my grandmother's wooden rocking chair and before I know it, my body is beckoned. Sitting down in the chair, its old wooden charms creak under my added weight, but the curves of the wood don't buckle under the pressure. Memories of her reading downstairs in the library dance behind my closed eyelids, invoking a wave of calmness, a sense of familiarity throughout my body. When I first came to live here as a child, I was quiet, closed off, and struggling developmentally. Kids would make fun of me because I had difficulties reading and stumbled over my words. Within the walls of this home, she taught me some of the mysteries and tales packed between the pages of books. The endless amount of journeys that lay behind a decorated cover. I learned how to stand up for myself and fight to be the woman she knew I would become.

As my mind recollects all of my most treasured fragments of time, a lone tear escapes and delicately slides down the skin of my cheek. Just one. A final tear in remembrance and celebration of the life she lived.

As the moments pass, embracing such dear memories, the sun's rays shift from stretching across my face to illuminating the darkest corner of the attic. Shining proudly under the light, I realize I have stumbled upon my grandmother's steamer trunk. Made of solid black aged wood, steel hardware, and leather strap handles, I know it contains unspoken stories of my grandmother's life.

She warned me never to rummage in her belongings and I followed through with that promise. It wasn't until after her death when I had no other choice, since she left me this home and all of her belongings in her will. This chest is one of many secrets my grandmother withheld from me. The strongest urge tells me that this trunk holds more than just her untold stories and it went to the grave with her.

Curiosity gets the best of me, so I decide without thinking, to smash the locks off the front panel to reveal what is hidden. More dust and foul air shoot upward into my face and nasal passages, inciting involuntary constriction from my lungs. Rapid-fire sneezes generate barring no warning, sending snot into my lap. I tuck the bottom half of my face, just below my eyes into the neck of my t-shirt, flailing my arms around to swat away the remaining particles floating in the air. Digging through the piles, I find private key-locked journals, what appear to be handwritten love notes, and a binder containing newspaper clippings in every inch of the chest. Yet only one thing at the bottom catches my eye—an antique, tarnished gold medallion.

Transfixed by the remaining gold sheen and the elaborate filigree, there isn't a single item in the chest that can tear me away from this one perplexity. A wild smile stretches across my face from ear to ear as an electrifying tingle charges up my spine. Resting in the center of the medallion is the most irresistible crimson gem I have ever seen. Enthralled by its beauty and how magnificent it feels under my caressing touch, I sense myself getting lost, drowning in the depths of its enigmatic pull. My mind searches through the memories of my life, highlighting moments where this artifact might have made an appearance. However, I fail to recollect anything of significance. Shattered pieces from my childhood fight to recall from a very young age the days before my grandfather was found guilty. There weren't many of them, but blurry, disordered tatters remain.

Under the firm touch of my fingers embrace, sharpened spikes from the medallion jet outward, slicing cleanly through flesh, narrowly missing the bones of my left hand. At first, I feel nothing, stunned by the violent intrusion, but as my blood quickly saturates my hand and pours down my forearm, the receptors regulating pain transcend comprehension.

Insurmountable anguish threatens to consume me in its grasp and my eyelids fight to remain open, my conscience fading rapidly. Yanking my t-shirt off as fast as my faltering strength allows, I wrap it around my hand in earnest, applying heavy pressure to stop the steady stream of blood flowing from the wound. Breaths come rapid and thready from my chest while I attempt to navigate to unsteady feet. Distorted, red-stained floorboards sway dangerously in my vision. I can make out the hazy image of my cell phone close to the door where I left it, but as I go to take my first step, my right foot slides through the viscous pool of blood lying beneath me. I'm left with little reaction time before my body crashes to the ground. The impact sends a jolt of pain shooting through my skull, momentarily blacking out my vision, and a thrust of numbness down into my limbs.

Consumed by the disorienting turmoil tearing through me, I'm barely able to curl onto my side in a fetal position, using my arms to cradle my head. The heady scent of blood and sweat fills my nose as my face becomes soaked in more of my life essence, telling me signs of the severity of my injury. I start to rock back and forth with the hope of mustering up enough strength to pull through and make a call for help. Grunts of frustration escape my lips as I shimmy each inch of movement toward my phone. Stings from sliver pieces of the raw wood beneath me slice into my exposed flesh, eliciting sharp intakes of breath and short, hissing inhales.

Bracing for a final push of power, I make it across the attic floor and click the emergency button on my lock screen. Relief washes over me at the sound of the operator's voice.

I've done it, help is coming.

⚰

THE DISTANT SOUNDS OF THE EMERGENCY VEHICLE SIRENS ARE THE last clear thing I remember while drifting in and out of consciousness. Muffled, hurried voices of the paramedics inundate me with questions; hazy images of riding in the back of the ambulance are nothing but cloudy leftover memories now. Even the pain seems to be something of my imagination, and the more I try to go back to that day, the images take on a foggier shape.

After numerous stitches on my hand and forehead, extensive monitoring, and a blood transfusion, I signed myself out of the hospital after a twenty-four-hour stay. However, since I was treated at the hospital where I work, there was no escaping the fact that my supervisors knew what happened and forced me to stay home for a few days. I tried to explain that I was fully capable of returning to work, but I lost that fight rather quickly. Leaving the hospital of my own volition and against medical advice doesn't grant me access to undermine the head of my department.

Aside from the necessary antibiotics, I refuse to fill the prescription for painkillers and plan to take an over-the-counter pain reliever instead. I want to heal my body, not be in a drug-induced state only to come out addicted to something I didn't want in the first place. It shouldn't be hard for a doctor to listen to his patient's refusal, especially one he works alongside, and still, he wrote the stupid prescription anyway. Stubborn, I know, but ask anyone, and they will tell you that caring for a medical professional is one of the hardest things to do because we are exceptionally hard-headed and firm in our beliefs of what we do and don't want to subject unto our bodies.

Stepping out of my local pharmacy, I throw open my arms, lean my head back to face the sun, and appreciate the lovely fall weather. A little sweater is all you need to stay comfortable, even though the first few weeks of the season have blown by. Hovering on the edge between summer and fall, the contradicting weather patterns harmonize magnifi-cently to form rare days of impeccability.

As silly as my accident may have been, I must not forget the severity of my circumstances and the high potential I could have bled out in that attic. Avoiding getting buried under morbid thoughts, I settle in the driver's seat of my Jeep and dig my phone out of my backpack. It's about time I reached out to my best friend.

After a few rings, the sweetest voice comes from the other line. "Hey, girl! Where've you been? I haven't heard from you in a few days." Kyla's usual tone is always drenched in happiness and excitement, except this time it's paired with a hint of worry behind the last phrase.

Having a lifelong bestie doesn't mean we have to talk every single day, but when a few days pass without a word, it's easy to notice. Usually one of us will break the silence, and this time, it's me. Subconsciously, we keep a binder stored in our minds of everything we need to catch each other up on. I hate that I never reached out while in the hospital, even though it wasn't intentional. I'm hoping a hot cup of tea and a brand-new book might ease her stress a bit.

"Kyla, before you freak out, I'm going to need you to take a few slow breaths, then I'll tell you."

Immediately, the volume of her voice lowers and the pacing of her response speeds up. "Are you okay, Bek? What happened?"

"Well, you see…" I pause, cautiously drawing out my words, "I may have done something stupid." My words cut right to the chase, yet only partially confess the truth.

"Rebekah Ann Musing, what did you do?" she yells back immediately.

"First off, this phone call is evident enough to claim that I am clearly fine, and you don't have to worry. I was in the hospi—"

She doesn't let me complete my sentence before hijacking the conversation. "The what?! I know you are not about to say you were in the hospital."

An uncontrollable laugh bursts from me. "Calm down, knucklehead, let me explain. On my days off, I've been clearing out my grandmother's old house floor by floor. Well, when I got to the attic I ended up finding her old steamer trunk and smashed my way inside."

"Okay, so how does this correlate to you being in the hospital?" she asks sardonically.

"Don't you start. If you'd hold for just a moment, you'd hear that I am getting to that part."

"*Hmph.*"

"Inside the trunk, I found the craziest and most intriguing, solid gold medallion I have ever seen. It didn't like me messing with it too much because while I held it in my grasp, it unlatched and almost amputated a few of my fingers."

"Oh my gosh, are you okay?!" Kyla shrieks loudly.

"Hold on, like I told you a moment ago, I am okay. I just wanted to call and check in, since I inadvertently ghosted you for a bit. I'm sorry girl."

As if pondering my apology, the other line goes quiet for a minute. "No matter how annoyed I am with you for not keeping me informed, I am relieved to know you are okay. You owe me though," Kyla finally responds, her tone more relaxed.

Relief of understanding from my best friend gives me a spark of renewed energy. "Well, how does tea and a new release sound?"

"It sounds like you are one step away from earning my forgiveness," she says, adding a heaping dose of snarkiness to her response.

"You got it, anything for you. Give me twenty minutes and I'll see you at your place."

"Deal."

A quick set of goodbyes, and I'm rolling down the road, windows down, to the place that keeps me smiling... the bookstore.

8

ONE WEEK AGO

Tonight is my first evening shift back to work after spending a week at home recovering from my accident. I decided that staying at my apartment was the smarter choice because I would be closer to the hospital if my condition changed and needed emergency support again. Secretly, I don't feel I am ready and healed enough to return to my grandmother's house quite yet.

Treating patients suffering from severe injuries is much easier for me because my mind shields itself and allows me to do my job effectively with precision. There is no shield when it is your own blood that you're scrubbing off the floors, untreatable stains mocking a traumatic experience. Remembering the devastation my hand wound caused sends an unnerving shiver down my spine at the thought of

67

returning to the attic. Sitting up from my recliner, I make a conscious effort to shake away any thought that isn't centered around my shift.

Being cooped up for a week is not how I typically enjoy spending my time. Regardless, I have to admit that it wasn't as terrible as I thought it would be. When I returned home from Kyla's the other day, I didn't trust myself behind the wheel of a vehicle until I was more recovered. I informed my overprotective friend of my whereabouts and then cocooned myself in my apartment.

Relaxing on my couch, binge-watching TV shows, and eating ice cream out of the container was an unexpected gift I didn't know I needed. In spite of it being a nice reprieve, I ponder whether I'm ready to head back to work. Subsequently, the report only said a mild concussion, which means I shouldn't be too worried about any medical mishaps that could potentially happen. I mean, if anything does happen, it's not like I'll be far. However, it is a bit early to remove the stitches, leaving me with apprehension and concern about being able to have full mobility of my hand. My mind wavers back and forth over whether I am making the correct decision. There is nothing to prove by returning to work so soon. I simply think I need to feel useful and get back to taking care of others instead of wallowing in self-pity.

Gathering a fresh set of folded scrubs from my laundry basket, I shuffle my way into the bathroom to prepare myself for the long shift awaiting me in the ED. I've been a nurse for ten years and somehow, putting on my uniform invokes a brand new sense of nervousness. The few short days I have been away have in some way shaken my confidence, leaving a strong feeling of unease behind. I feel like an imposter deemed unworthy to don the signature navy blue attire for my department. Doubt tiptoes in the back of my mind, spreading viciously like a blazing wildfire.

Brushing my long hair up into a bun, a quick peek in the reflection of the mirror stops my movements abruptly. I know I lost a lot of blood, however, the person staring back at me stands in a corpse-like ghostly pallor. My natural porcelain appearance borders transparent, with bruises dispersed down my arms, my chest, and up the anterior part of my neck. Sunken cheeks and somber eyes create an image of pensive sadness.

Whistling howls from increasing winds outside snap my attention away from the somber atmosphere surrounding me. Another glance back in the mirror reflects the normal, healthy image I'm accustomed to seeing. Averting my gaze away from the glass, I swiftly shut off the light and bolt out of the bathroom. Shaken up from the unexplainable events in the mirror, I hastily grab my phone, water jug, my work bag I prepared earlier, and exit my apartment as fast as my feet will allow.

Hopping in my black Jeep Wrangler, I slam the door shut and pound my fists against the steering wheel. Raw, aggravated screams echo around me in the limited space. The thought of being in my apartment at this moment is out of the question. I *have* to go to work. Drowning out my disordered thoughts, I hit shuffle on my metal playlist and blast it louder than my speakers or my eardrums deem appropriate. At this moment, I don't care about causing damage, I need to make whatever is causing this unexplainable activity to stop its torment.

Speeding dangerously around narrow turns and drifting haphazardly over the double yellow lines, I surprisingly make it to the hospital's employee lot in one piece. Thankfully, there was no one else on the road, or I would have perilously and illegally passed them. No amount of distance away from my apartment makes me feel safe right now. Rounding the bend and seeing the old building I call my second home brings forth spreading calmness. Parking in my usual spot under a large oak tree, I lean my head back against the headrest, take one last full breath, grab my gear, and head inside.

Walking in via the ambulance bay automatic doors, I am greeted by my favorite evening security guard. Sporting a full head of white hair and a plump round belly, Ron has been dutifully monitoring the halls of this hospital since before I was born. The right man for the job when the moon is full and the witching hour sets the ED ablaze.

"Hey Bek, good to have you back. How you feelin'?" Ron asks, displaying a genuine smile and comforting pat on my back.

Gently nudging him in his side, I quip back with a chuckle, "Awe, don't tell me you were worried about me, old man."

"Oh, don't you start that foolishness now. I'm always worried about you, Bek. I shouldn't have to remind you of that after all these years. I promised your grandmother I'd always keep a watchful eye over you and that is what I'm doing." Ron tilts his head down and flashes me a tiny wink. That little bit of movement lets me see the worry etched in his brow and the despair behind his eyes, no matter how hard he tries to cover it up.

I don't want him to see the distress on my face, therefore I school my facial features and leave him with reassurance that I am doing alright.

"I know you're just looking out for me because you care. I'm fine, I promise. It was only a small accident, you have nothing to worry about." My tone hitches higher than my usual alto, however, his face doesn't indicate that he noticed the falsity of my statement. Lying to someone I hold near and dear, flips my stomach upside down.

Taking the pad of his index finger, he lightly dabs the tip of my nose and gives me another wink. "You come directly to me if that changes."

"Yeah, yeah, you got it," I reply, half-heartedly shooing him away, while simultaneously closing the break room door in his face. Throwing my belongings in my locker, I try to forget about being dishonest to Ron and remind myself that it's for his own good that he stays clear of what is happening to me.

How do you explain events that have no name or explanation?

Checking my room assignments on the whiteboard, I get started stocking my cart right away. Ignoring my problems and focusing my time and energy on my patients allows me to compartmentalize and acknowledge that my issues pale in comparison.

Day shift had no patients to transfer over, so the start of my shift sails pretty smoothly. As the night slithers on by, the injuries and illnesses have thankfully been non-life-threatening. A six-year-old who thought jumping on his bed was a smart idea, went home in a soft cast on his forearm and orders to see an orthopedic doctor for a hard cast. Two quick admissions to our inpatient psychiatric unit for stabilization and a plethora of headaches, abdominal distress, and minor suture needs.

Glancing up from my charts, I notice day shift gracing us with their bright-eyed and bushy-tail faces. I can't remember the last time a shift went this smoothly. Transferring my patients over without any issues, I say my quick goodbyes to the day shift nurses and stroll out to my vehicle, a bit more pep in my step this time around.

An uneventful night surely makes up for the terrible day I had yesterday. I feel so much better after getting out of the house and going to work. A powerful feeling of accomplishment wraps around me tightly and gives me the energetic boost I need. Jumping back in my Jeep, I leisurely make my way home, paying extra attention to how the warm rays of the rising sun caress my skin and cast striking patterns on the leaves of the trees.

Approaching my apartment complex, a metaphorical dark cloud seems to hover over my unit, stealing any remnants of happiness. Regardless of the rays, the warm air around me is replaced by a cold breeze brushing along my skin and sinks to my bones. All positive feelings, confidence, and mindful thoughts, quickly fade away with each hesitant step further toward my apartment.

Subconsciously, I avoid the elevator and take the stairs up to the third floor. The closer I get to my place, the heavier the uneasiness weighs against my body. Belief that I can turn around and run away from this place fades away soon after appearing, as if my mind rejected the idea before fully developing.

Opening my apartment door unleashes a new layer of anxiety. Apprehension of being alone right now expedites the erosion of stability on my sanity. Scanning my eyes across my open-layout home, nothing out of the ordinary pops out at me. Apart from the overconsumption of physical books stacking up in random piles, I try my very best to keep my living space nice and tidy. No dishes piling in the sink, or take-out containers overflowing from my trash bin. There isn't even dust on the various photo frames of my grand-mother and I.

My favorite captured moment of us sits squarely in the center of my walnut coffee table. The photo was taken by Ron, our closest family friend, a few years after my mother was murdered. During the peak months of fall, my grandmother and I were encapsulated in time making leaf angels under my favorite red maple tree. Radiant smiles are preserved in a memory that I will never forget.

Glancing at the photo, I am reminded of how strong and resilient my grandmother used to be. This simple photograph washes away some of the unexplained dread consuming me. Avoiding having to enter my bathroom, I grab the spare toothbrush, face wash, and hairbrush out of my work bag and wash up in my kitchen sink. Taking my mental well-being into consideration, I consciously choose not to walk in the room that began this breakdown almost twenty-four hours ago.

Washed up, changed, and ready for bed, I grab the top book on my nightstand and nestle snugly under the covers. A cute, easy-to-read, romantic comedy is what I need to shake away my stress before closing my eyes and drifting off to sleep.

Resting on a bench outside of my local cafe, the warmth of the sun's fleeting rays melts along the right side of my face and neck. Magnificent hues on the horizon airbrush a seamless blend of magenta, coral, and gold, casting unique patterns from behind the wall of trees circling the town center. The heavenly aroma wafting out of the white paper bag holding a hot, mouthwatering, cinnamon muffin topped with handmade cream cheese icing, flutters to my empty stomach. Tranquility wraps me in its gentle breeze.

Breaking off a piece of the sweet indulgence, deafening screams shatter the perfect dreamscape, causing me to drop the morsel on the sidewalk. Shadows steal the sun's illumination, blanketing myself and everything surrounding me in darkness. Serenity is snuffed out and replaced with burdening terror, heightening my anxiety and pulse. A brisk chill elicits vulnerable shudders down my body and lasting goosebumps on my flesh.

Searching frantically for the source of the noise, I am dumbfounded to find no one close to me shows any signs of distress or worry.

Darting over to the older gentleman walking his husky, I step in sync with his quickened pace. "Excuse me, Sir, do you have any idea where that scream came from?"

Stopping unexpectedly at my question, he slowly cranks his head down to look me in the eye. Instead of seeing the face of a man, I am greeted by two hollowed-out eye sockets and an unnatural, animated grin. Jumping back, I collide with the metal cage holding a trash can in place and crash to the ground. Savage laughter bellows from the face of the terrorizing man. Scurrying to my feet, I don't hesitate sprinting in the opposite direction away from the haunting figure.

The once-deserted sidewalk fills with faceless apparitions of those I recognize from my local area, spilling into the vacant street. Vicious cackles explode from all directions, drowning me in a blackened sea of desperation.

Booming rumbles of thunder and crashing branches against my window startle me awake in a pool of sweat. Thunderstorms are my favorite weather, but immediately I notice something uniquely unsettling filling the air. My hand reaches out to find an unseen, dense presence looming in front of me. Mere seconds after my eyes flick open, a bolt of lightning saturates the bedroom in flashes of light. Disoriented and confused, black circles dance across my eyesight, impairing my vision temporarily. An unexpected gap in my blackout curtains exposes frequent battles of illumination. As each pulse lights up my bedroom, the sound of my quickening breaths leaving my lungs floods my ears. Goosebumps suddenly cover my skin, raising the hair on my forearms and the back of my neck. Powerful, electrifying nerve impulses quickly release, causing my body to shudder involuntarily under the covers.

Pulling myself upright against the support of my headboard, my heart rate rapidly speeds up, thumping intensely within the walls of my chest. All at once, the chaotic energy around me seizes its unstoppable assault. I know for certain now that I am no longer alone.

"Hello, little fox."

9

Rayna

Breaking through our heavy conversation, the obnoxious rear entrance door alarm snaps us both back to reality. Regardless of the conundrum we are trying to piece together, we still have a job to perform. Until we know more, the smartest course of action is to remain quiet and keep our theories to ourselves. Hell, at this point how do I believe this story myself? Sleep deprivation alone could be the cause of my cognitive impairment and delusions. If only the skull-crushing pain would subside, I could sit down and unravel this endless mystery.

Using his large, domineering frame, Sgt. Hamlin barrels through the double doors, shoving the defenseless techs bringing in the transport stretcher out of the way. Barely one step out of my office and I'm bombarded with his frustration.

"Please tell me this is a suicide and not another victim to add to this killer's body count."

This man has obviously lost his mind if he thinks he can come into *my* lab and start demanding answers and dictating how I'm doing *my* job. "You know I can't dismissively label it a suicide without doing a proper examination."

The dumbfounded expression on his face tells me he was unprepared for my rebuttal and did not like the surprise he got from my backboned audacity. This isn't our first time working together, so he should know by now that I refuse to bow down to his "authority." His chest heaves from the heaviness of his breathing and his nares flare in irritation.

"I mean, it's pretty cut and dry, don't you think? A large gash like that *clearly* looks self-inflicted. You don't need to be a genius or medical expert to figure that out," his volume spikes on each word, showing a lack of emotional control.

Scoffing at his words, I can't help the smirk growing on my face. "And that is where *you* are wrong. *I'm*—" I sneer, pointing a finger at my chest, "—the medical expert, and I haven't yet examined the body. So no, you're not getting the cause of death until I thoroughly complete the autopsy according to procedural protocol and conclude my findings, Sergeant Hamlin."

"Jack, come on man, talk some sense into this woman!" Sergeant Hamlin's fury and nonexistent patience now fully overtook his features. Seething rage burns behind his eyes, accompanied by the faint rush of red tinting on his skin and a near-constant throb of the frontal vein down the center of his forehead.

"How dare—'' Words barely form on my lips when Jack steps directly in between us to ease the growing tension. Strong, firm hands press against mine and Sergeant assholes breastbones, strictly keeping us from tearing into each other further. Jack is well-versed in how I operate and knows that there is no backing down when the integrity of my career is on the line.

"Look Sarge, this isn't the first time that we have been called in on one of your cases. You know just as well as I do that she is the best in the field and will get to the bottom of things—we both will. Rayna, please go over there and cool off, we can talk about this in a minute." Jack's eyes plead for me to listen and tame my rage.

Sergeant Hamlin's overinflated ego prevents him from keeping his mouth shut and having the last word. "I don't have to reiterate how important it is to catch this bastard. The last thing we need is for extra resources going towards this death when there could be more potential victims out there. Let's not waste time on this one," he argues, snapping the back of his right hand into the palm of his left, emphasizing his words.

Lingering tension vibrates through the air, leaving it charged and thick from our argument. However, two things I know for certain. One, Jack usually never calls me by my first name, especially in that tone unless he is without a doubt done with dealing with my shit. And two, Jack doesn't get angry... ever. He has an endless supply of patience, which means that in roughly twenty-five years of friendship, I can count on one hand how many times he has been angry or disappointed in my actions. Maybe I have pushed the boundary a bit too far this time.

Only a few inches separate the height difference between these two men, thankfully leaning in favor of Sgt. Hamlin being taller. I am unsure if his insecure masculinity can take another hit this evening while he is under this much stress— or any time for that matter. I might not fully understand men and their strange behaviors, but it doesn't take someone with my educational knowledge to know the Sgt. is a prideful man and isn't one for things not going his way. Having a large structured frame leaves little room for someone to not feel intimidated in his presence, but he doesn't scare me.

Placing a firm, yet friendly arm across the broad shoulders of the Sergeant, Jack leads them both casually in the direction of the exit, inaudibly murmuring between themselves. Employing a bit of Jack's infamous charm and charisma, the palpable tension surrounding them dissipates quickly. Smiles and laughter paint their faces, slicing through the former tension-coated air seamlessly.

I glance over at the techs who stopped midway between the back doors to watch the slow downhill spiral of the Sergeant and their boss become heated over a case. I'm sure they got great enjoyment out of catching their supervisor, who is smart enough to dominate in a medical field, yet can't even remember their names, become unhinged with the police Sergeant. One of these days when we don't have a serial killer out there, I will remember their names, but I don't think today will be that day. Besides, most of our technicians are only here for a school semester, or leave early because I inadvertently scare them away. Typically, they gravitate toward Jack's charismatic and infectious personality, avoiding me as much as possible.

While Jack strokes the over-inflated confidence of Sgt. Hamlin, I motion with my hands for the two female techs to return their attention back to the corpse on the transport stretcher. "Can you ladies take Ms. Musing and prepare her for examination, please?"

Slowly dragging her gaze from Jack's direction, the taller brunette rolls her eyes at me before huffing out a clipped response. "Sure."

I have plenty of reasons to believe they'd like to stay and watch Jack in all his glory, but this isn't the time and place. A man's behavior is usually repulsive and abhorrent, however, these women have their eyes locked on Jack. He is rather handsome, in a unique, yet almost unconventional way, so I don't blame them. But I've never looked at Jack as more than a brother.

Contrary to everything I've said about emotions and how they are a waste of time, Jack always manages to have the magic touch to break through the invisible wall caging in that part of me. The secret password if you will, to unlock the box containing my hidden innermost depths. Unwilling to admit it out loud, or even to him, I do find solace in his presence—a protector for all of the vulnerable and raw pieces.

Finding comfort in the morgue is not a common occurrence for most. For me, this is where I can thrive in my quest for the truth and potentially save innocent lives from becoming future victims. Where one finds safety and mental ease wrapped in a cozy blanket on the couch, or enjoying a book on the beach, I find my time spent in this frigid environment rather soothing. My cloak of comfort is the unforgettable scent of formaldehyde permeating the mortuary air, the ability to focus on my work without interruptions, and the confirmation that our diligent ethic sends the sick and sadistic to rot behind bars.

There was no one to stand up for me when I was a child, no one to protect me from the dangers in my own home. My older sisters were able to escape our father's torment and left me to suffer alone. Catastrophe came at the expense of my mother's life and I refuse to sit around idly without seeking the answers that once failed my family. The Sergeant tried to claim a territory that he knows nothing about and I'm not going to sit back and watch him do it.

Chemicals and cleaning supplies marred with a faint hint of death embrace me in open arms, a small moment of reprieve at a time like this. Disregarding the last few moments that recently occurred, I'm left dangerously to my thoughts. Awareness of who is lying in the black body bag returns in full force. I owe my full concentration and professional capabilities to Rebekah. Conflicting with what the angry Sergeant concluded, I refuse to accept this young woman's life ended devoid of purpose. Speculations don't find killers and leave the door to the truth unopened. Countless possibilities could explain what we saw today at the crime scene, but it is up to Jack and I to find the last remaining piece to complete the mystery.

Lost in my thoughts and documentation files, Jack's footsteps are almost inaudible in his approach from behind. His reflection on my computer screen gave away his proximity, otherwise I probably would have jumped out of my chair.

"Care to explain what all of that was about?" His accusatory tone holds mixed tones of annoyance and sarcasm.

"I'm pretty sure I made myself clear," I retort quickly, refusing to turn my head away from my computer screen.

Out of the corner of my eye on the edge of my peripheral, I notice Jack shift into a defensive yet relaxed position, leaning against the edge of my desk. "I'm not crucifying you here, I just want to know what happened to my friend and why she allowed someone like him to get under her skin. You're better than that. He doesn't deserve to see you unravel. Get back at him by proving once again that we are the best team he has."

I pause briefly, his wording throwing me slightly off guard. Seconds later, I dramatically roll my head to the side and shoot my eyes up over my glasses. I give him a half-hearted response, "Can I blame it on lack of sleep?"

"*Yeeeaah*, I don't think that's how it works. Until this case is over, can you at least pretend to play nice with the police?"

"Only on one condition. Sergeant Macho isn't allowed back in this lab until this case is solved."

Hesitating, Jack quickly extends his right pinky in my direction, "Promise?"

"Fine," I huff loudly. "Pinky promise."

Growing up, Jack didn't have any siblings, but never exhibited signs commonly found among those that grow up as an only child. We always had each other to rely on and when it was time for a promise, the pinky was always the truest test of friendship and trust. A pinky promise solidified that the other person was going to be there for you no matter what. You never break pinky promises, so for Jack's sake and the little girl hidden deep inside me, I'll try to be on my best professional behavior.

"Whatcha workin' on?" His quick directional change in the conversation sends my thoughts through a whirlwind searching for clarity.

"I'm trying to finish my documentation of the field assessment today. The techs are in the other room preparing Rebekah if you want to go check on them. I'm sure they'd *love* to have your assistance." My words escape involuntarily, robotic and a bit snarky.

Still propped against the edge of my desk, Jack gazes down at me, a look of concern crossing his features. He waits for my full attention before continuing. "Are you sure you're okay working on her tonight? I have no problem taking the lead on this so you can go home and get some proper rest."

Flipping uncontrollably like a light switch, my emotions rapidly change unexpectedly and lack intentional provocation. "I can't believe this! After all these years, you're doubting my capabilities now?"

Instinctually, Jack firmly but not painfully holds down my shoulder, foiling my attempt to spring from my chair and firing more nonsense at him. When he speaks, his voice is calm and direct, leaving no room for interpretation. "Ray, please don't be like this. You're running on little to no sleep, you've been running yourself ragged since this case started, and you can't shake these nightmares. I'm not doubting your capabilities, I am simply offering you a moment of peace."

Before responding, I close my eyes to remind myself who I'm speaking with. I am smart enough to understand his concerns and how he's correct in acknowledging my extreme lack of sleep. After a few deep breaths, I'm composed enough to carry on the conversation. "I *have* to do this, Jack. I am being targeted on this case for a reason. Just to refresh your memory," I spear my arm in the direction of the mortuary coolers, "you do realize that I look pretty damn similar to those victims laying in the refrigerator right now. This case is connected to me somehow and I can't help but feel responsible for those that are at risk because they look similar to me." Choking on my words, I ask the question that's been haunting me all afternoon. "Why is this happening to me?"

Jack hops off my desk to spin me around in my chair and face him directly. Kneeling in front of me, he rests his hands in mine and tenderly rubs the back side of my hand, avoiding the wrapped sutures. "I wish I had answers to your questions. I am in the dark as much as you. No one is going to look at you differently for not being able to carry this one through to the end. You hear me? No one. You're not alone Ray, I've got you."

"Stop it. You don't get to decide what is best for me," I reply weakly, my voice lacking any semblance of strength and avoiding eye contact. My compromised mental fortitude crumbles in seconds and tears threaten to fall. I feel raw and exposed for the second time today, even in the face of someone who I cherish and admire. I don't know how to deal with the constant shift of my emotions. The last few days have shown me some of the most mentally difficult challenges I have faced.

As a lone tear escapes the confines of my restraint, Jack gently swipes it off my cheek using his thumb and speaks at a volume only I can hear, "It's okay."

"*Ahem.*" Neither one of us noticed when the technicians returned from the back prepping area. The last thing I can afford to think about is someone overhearing the fragility of my current state of mind and questioning my capabilities for this case.

Averting their gaze away from me, the taller tech speaks directly to Jack as if I am not sitting next to him or even present in the room. "Ms. Musing is all prepped and ready for examination."

"Alright, thanks, Gianna. You and Olivia can gather your stuff and head home for tonight, we can take it from here," Jack replies, paying little mind to their flirtatious body language.

"You sure? If Dr. Pierce needs to leave, we are more than happy to assist you," Gianna responds, a touch of seduction mixed in her tone.

"Nope, you ladies have done enough today. Get on outta here," Jack says, leaving no room for interpretation.

Both young women roll their eyes before sending a glare in my direction, clearly unsatisfied that Jack is oblivious to their attention-seeking behavior. Once they are out of earshot, he returns his focus back to me. Leaning over my chair, Jack grips the armrests resting close to my thighs.

Fierce cobalt eyes lock onto mine. "I'm not leaving any room for debate. I'm making sure you get some food, taking you home, and tucking you into bed."

As much as I want to fight him, I know this is a losing battle, so I'm going to take this temporary loss and save what remaining strength I have left. This week is far from over.

"You know, that actually sounds like a great idea. It's late anyway, so getting sleep is probably for the best."

IO

IT DIDN'T TAKE MUCH CONVINCING FROM JACK TO LEAVE THE
morgue early tonight and take me home.

Mentally, I have exhausted myself far beyond words can
express, and physically, my body is incapable of healing until
I get some much-needed rest. The past forty-eight hours
have been an aggressive vortex of destruction suctioning my
life toward a disastrous black hole. Are there words to
describe how this case has affected me? Probably not,
however, a vacation of some type or at least some time away
from work is definitely needed. I'm not sure if I will ever
admit this to him, but he is right, I am not well right now. I
need food and a proper night's sleep before continuing with
this case.

After locking up, Jack and I quietly make our way to his

car. The air around us doesn't feel tense, yet I can sense he wants to continue our earlier conversation from my office, while also allowing me space and time to process. Combining the blasting heat and rock softly playing in the background, I catch myself dozing off to the sounds of Jack singing—poorly I might add—but more so to the feeling of safety and comfort. It takes a lot of trust for me to fall asleep around someone. Although I know if something were to happen while I slept, I am in good hands. Through my sleep-filled haze, I can see a distinct shade of a yellow light cast off in the distance. It is a bit out of the way, except he knows that chicken nuggets and a crisp soda from my favorite fast food joint are exactly what I need after a really tough day. Within a few minutes without having to tell him, my "fix everything" comfort meal that my mom used to sneak up to my bedroom is now in my hands.

The unforgettable greasy, salty smell of hot french fries permeates the air in Jack's car, sending my stomach into a frenzy. "Thank you," I mumble, while shoving the delicious golden potatoes in my mouth. Savoring the mouthful, the unforgettable flavors send my mind tumbling back in a memory.

Clutching my childhood teddy to my chest and cupping my ear with my hand, I try to hide my breathing so my father doesn't know I am hiding under my bed. It makes me uncomfortable to be in the house when he yells at my mother. Loud voices, objects flying, and broken furniture hurts my ears. Mom is always so distraught when they fight around us because I know she feels helpless she can't save us from this environment. I think my sisters are lucky enough this time to be outside right now and can't hear their argument. A loud bang from the front door stops their shouting downstairs in the living room. I don't know who stormed off this time, so I wait under my bed until I know it is safe for me to come out.

Creaking on the steps alerts me someone is coming, so I take a deep breath and hold it in for as long as I can. "Ray, my little sunshine. Are you up here?" my mother's sweet voice calls out.

Sliding out from underneath the bed, an older version of me sits cross-legged on the carpet near my door. Tears have stopped running down her cheeks, but her eyes are swollen and I see a new split in her bottom lip. Resting in her lap is a bag containing the meal she always says will fix everything. It isn't often I get to have it, so when I do she strokes my hair and reminds me that everything will be alright. No matter what, I always believe her.

"For what?" Jack questions with an arch of his brow and a straw sticking out the corner of his mouth.

Shaking away the painful memory from when I was roughly ten years old, I mask the tone of my voice and carry on with the conversation as if nothing occurred. "Oh, you know, reminding me that I can't survive on a cup of coffee and persistently reassuring me that it is okay to be human."

Reaching over the center console, Jack latches onto my leg above my knee and gives me a soothing stroke with his thumb. "It's my job, silly. You're mine to watch over and protect, even if you refuse to accept protection and tell me to fuck off all the time."

"Well, that isn't going to change! I do very much appreciate you, you're not allowed to forget that."

Arriving back at my apartment, the intense call from my bed makes me comply with Jack's request to walk me to my door. If he worries any harder, I'm afraid his head is going to start spinning with smoke billowing from his ears. Living in the mountains means that there aren't many things I need to be afraid of, although that changes when there is a serial killer at large. To a certain extent, I can't fault him for being cautious.

Pausing at my front door, Jack gives me a familiar look I know all too well. I can tell by his expression that this evening's antics of overprotection have yet to come to a conclusion. Giving him a playful shove on the shoulder, I shake my head at his constant need to watch over me. "I'm not letting you walk me inside, so I'm saying goodnight now and letting you go home to rest your bones."

"But—"

"Absolutely not! We are not thirteen, you can't come in and tuck me in."

"You always have to take the fun out of everything, don't you," he scoffs theatrically, stomping his foot playfully in a childish manner.

"Goodnight, Jack. I'll see you in the morning," I chuckle, shoving him out of the doorway and toward his vehicle.

Practically shutting the door in his face, I leave no room to hear his final words of the evening or any other advice he wants to throw my way. As soon as I hear the solid click of my deadbolt, I collapse my body against the back of the door, and let out a breathy sigh, dropping all of my belongings at my feet. Instinctually, I stare down at the heap surrounding my feet on the floor. The physical weight of my day is summed up by a few heavy duffle bags while the psychological burden rests heavily on my mind and shoulders. Cleaning up my clutter from the day is now a problem for future me because I can't be bothered to put it away right now.

Releasing such overloaded breaths eases the tightness in my chest and drops my shoulders into a more neutral position. This week has been hell, more specifically, the time between finding the fifth victim and now has been the most brutal. Stress is a toxic poison that wreaks havoc on the body. Eating away at our natural immune system, destroys functioning organ systems, and disrupts any balance internally. Parasitic feeding from the inside out.

Dragging myself to the bedroom, I fight the urge to collapse on my bed and sack out for the night, however, the need to wash away the day wins that battle. My legs don't have the strength to stand up long enough for a shower, so the call of a hot bath entices my aching muscles with the promise of pain relief. I don't often take enough time for myself, including self-care, thus a soothing bath is surely needed this evening. Shuffling my aching feet to the bathroom, I haphazardly throw my clothes on the floor with each step. Another addition of belongings to the disorder of my life and living quarters.

Setting the water temperature to scalding hot, I climb in straight away as the water fills the tub. I am not one to indulge in many frilly, highly fragranced things, but I do love bath salts and bubbles for my muscles. Sometimes indulging in the simple things can really make a difference.

Resting my head on the space where the wall meets the edge of my tub, I softly close my eyes and begin to center my thoughts. Heavy sighs continue to escape me as my body sinks lower into the scalding water. Old thoughts and memories surface at the idea of submerging my head under as well, fully escaping this reality for good. I keep my eyes closed and shift my mind to how the water feels against my skin. Tranquilizing heat penetrates deep through the layers of muscle and soothes the deep ache in my bones. Quiet crackles from the bubbles fill the silence following the water faucet shutting off. Soft notes of lavender and patchouli essential oils waft delicately to my nose, providing a great sense of mental relief.

"I finally have you all to myself. You have made this game a lot more interesting."

My eyes jolt open. "Hello? Is anyone there?" I inquire loudly, leaving no room for hesitation in my tone.

No response.

Holding my breath, I send all of my concentration into the darkness, listening intently for any disruption. Nothing returns.

Shifting back down into the water, I refuse to allow my suspicions to ruin the calm environment, so my ears stay vigilant for the return of the deep gravelly voice.

After a bit of time passing, my fingers and toes start to get wrinkly from the now chilly water forcing me to get out. Firmly wrapping the towel around my body, I walk over to the mirror and stare back at myself. Dark circles and dull, sunken eyes stare back at me. Faint wrinkle lines marr my face around my eyes, nose, and mouth. I'd prefer not to turn back the clock on my age, but I do wish a more jovial person painted my external features.

"You are enchanting, my Queen."

My hand shoots to the light switch dimmer, slamming it to the highest setting. Bright artificial illumination spreads to every corner of this small space, nearly blinding me in the process. My voice calls out, a slight quiver behind my words. "Is someone there? What the fuck do you want?"

Again, no answer.

My heart pounds against my ribcage, signaling rapid, shallow breathing from my lungs. If something were to happen to me, the last thing I want is to be found naked, so I grab the closest pair of clean lounge clothes and head out to investigate the mysterious voice further.

Reaching for my Louisville slugger, complete with a sock covering the barrel, I slide it from behind my dresser and bring it with me for extra oomph. I'm not one to get paranoid easily, but I don't recall ever hearing voices when I've neglected sleep to this extent. For added measure, I stealthily go around my apartment to make sure my front door is locked and my windows are well secured and the blinds are closed fully. As well protected as I feel in the woods, there is no denying that there is a serial killer out there who has a keen taste for those with red hair and fair skin. Once I've gone through my apartment and note nothing out of the ordinary, I make sure all the lights are off and ready myself to fight through the inevitable night terror set to destroy me.

Curling up in bed, I crash into my mountain of pillows, tug the blanket over my head, and keep my fingers crossed that a peaceful night's sleep envelops me. A feeble attempt to focus my eyes before darkness consumes me and throws me under the waves of the unknown. Soft cackling erupts in the deep canals of my ears before pulling my mind into the abyss.

Agonizing pain explodes through my ankle and wraps power-fully around the muscles and joints of my leg. Burning heat severs through every chain of thought. My right leg is set ablaze in a searing hot, fiery pain, while warm, viscous liquid runs down my lower leg and over my bare foot. Why am I not wearing any shoes?

Total darkness prevents my eyes from adjusting to see the destruction, but my instincts tell me I am back in the deepest parts of the woods. The smell of wet, damp dirt merges with a sharp smell of wood and rotting Earth. A soundless aether surrounds me, leaving me at a loss of one of my senses.

Trembling hands reach down hesitantly to find the source of my agony. An unknown pointed apparatus has closed around the thick muscle belly of my calf, slicing fragments of bone, and ripping savagely through my flesh with ease. Razor-sharp, serrated, metal teeth have penetrated through my lower leg, nearly severing it from the rest of my body. Inaudible screams rip through my lips. Indescribable pain fires off from every nerve ending still attached to my limb while electrical shocks tear through my nervous system for control. A waterfall of silent tears pours down my face.

Frantically unraveling, I attempt to drag my body through the dirt and leaves on the forest floor in hopes of finding a way out of this godforsaken place. Saturated terrain squelches under my panic-stricken palms, clawing fruitlessly through the murky underbrush. Each minuscule movement transmits insufferable waves of anguish barreling through me, freezing me in place.

The last time I felt its presence, it was right on top of me, closing the distance between us. Nearly immobile and confined to the forest floor, I swivel my head in all directions searching for the monster responsible. Where is it? Where is my enemy?

"Hello, my Queen," a gravelly, distorted voice calls to me from behind.

"What do you want from me? Leave me alone!" I shout into nothingness, still unable to make out the size and shape of my opponent. Snot, tears, and saliva cascade uncontrolled down my face and neck. I can feel my heart beating in the back of my throat and a surge of adrenaline pumping in my ears. The outcome of my survival is uncertain, but I know I have the determination to tackle this enemy. If this is to be my end, I will go down swinging.

"Tsk. Tsk. You thought you could escape me? I have been watching you for eons and I am done waiting. You are MINE, do you hear me?"

"I belong to no one!"

"That is where you are wrong. I am in control now. The King has finally captured his Queen, thanks to my loathsome little fox. She thought she was protecting everyone, and still, you fell right into the sticky web of the spider."

"I don't know what you're talking about."

A twig snaps mere inches from my sitting form, causing my whole body to jump further on edge. I know it's close, but I still can't see this shadowy figure.

Warm breath heavily scented in the smell of decay softly caresses up the back of my neck and across my face before receding quickly. "Think. Real hard. I thought you were smarter than this," it mocks. The dark and ominous voice continues to distort and reverberate off every tree close by, making it difficult to pinpoint where this foe is located. "Have you figured it out yet?"

"No, I haven't figured it out yet! I don't know what sick, demented game you're trying to play, but I want no part in it. Let me go, you sadistic piece of shit!"

"Oh, I love how feisty you are, it makes my mouth water."

When I refuse to further entertain its odd game of cat and mouse, I foolishly begin to believe it has given up and left me to die.

Just when I start to calm down and reassess my predicament, its haunting voice pierces through the forest. "I am going to release you now, so you better run. I can taste your fear on my tongue and might I say, you are richly decadent."

Without warning, the locked cage embedded in my flesh springs open, reigniting substantial amounts of torment. Fresh bursts of blood gush from the eviscerated tissue. Rapid gasps of breath rip from my struggling lungs, poorly attempting to remain conscious. Seconds tick by before the severity of my situation consumes my body and I am toppling face-first into the dirt.

Drowning in a sea of blackness, a muted female voice screams to me from a distance, "WAKE UP!"

II

TWO DAYS AGO

Jarring awake, a searing pain laces through each tissue layer of my torso and squeezes around my spinal cord. Guttural screams rip out of my throat as the sensation of tearing muscle fibers bend, twist, and writhe under my skin, causing extreme nausea. Quivering abdominal muscles fight to contain any remaining stomach acid and food left in my body. The intense beats of my heart flood my ears with an overwhelming rush of blood, robbing me of balance. Immense pressure builds from the inner walls of my rib cage and continues to squeeze until the right side of my chest cavity collapses. Bone-shattering pain shoots up my spine causing my back to lift off my mattress and contort uncontrollably.

Gathering what remaining strength I can, I throw my blankets off my body and to the other side of the bed, begging wordlessly for relief as molten heat soars through my skin, igniting to the bone. Sweat pours down my face, chest, and arms, soaking the sheets. The smallest of movements betray my stomach's hold, allowing bile to scorch my throat, and threatening to escape through clenched lips. Refusing to vomit, I swallow the burning, metallic-tasting contents back down and clamp a hand over my mouth as an extra precaution. Straining through swollen and tender eyelids, I notice the shadows and shapes of my room furniture, providing momentary reassurance of my surroundings until an aggressive wave of vertigo crashes directly into my minimal eyesight and throws me back against the stack of pillows.

Prioritizing my breathing, I close my eyes and coerce my body to rest calmly, taking back control from the violent moments of torment. Fragments of previous memories appear disjointed and blurry, barring no memories of climbing in bed last night. The last thing I remember is leaving my department and walking out to my Jeep, but the snippets of the final memory warp and fade into dark oblivion.

When I've reached a few moments of reprieve, I exhaust any residual power to sit up in bed. Concentrating fiercely on each movement, I open my eyes slowly, but the scene in front of me instantly threatens to destroy every last piece of calculated sanity. My former green sheets are coated in varying shades of blood and what appear to be fragments of human flesh and bits of unidentified meat. Frozen in place, my eyes travel from my sheets to my fully covered frame.

Violent tremors take over every muscle in my body as the

realization of my situation reforms in my head. My work scrubs and hospital ID badge clipped to my pocket are drenched in sticky, coagulated crimson, mixed together in layers of dried dirt and debris. No, no, no, this can't be happening, not again. Panic takes over and masks the pain previously devouring my body.

Springing from my bed, I take off running on the path to the bathroom, leaping over the piles of books scattered across my floor. Stumbling into the dark room, my hand flips the light switch to reveal the gravity of my situation in the full-length mirror. Staring at my reflection in utter shock, I quietly ask out loud, "What did you do this time?"

"*We got undeniably messy this time.*"

Squeezing my eyes shut and smashing my hands to my temples, I return a shout back to the hoarse voice hidden inside my mind. "Stop this madness! This is the fifth time I have woken up having zero recollection of what happened the previous evening. You toy with me all day while I am trying to sleep and then disappear for hours while I am at work. What do you want with me and why won't you allow me to remember?"

"*Oh little fox, I do not want you, you are just a pawn in the game to capture my Queen.*"

"I am no one's pawn! Tell me what you've done to me," I reply through clenched teeth.

"*Ah, ah, I do not think you are worthy of knowing what I have done using your face and body.*"

Reaching the limits of my already short leash of patience, I ram my clenched fist through the bathroom mirror, sending shards of broken glass scattering through the air. "TELL ME!"

Silence.

The quiet void of echoed stillness fills the small space of my bathroom and charges the air around me. Hairs along my exposed arms stand at attention, fighting through the dried blood coating my skin. I remain standing in front of my sink, glaring at the crimson-coated reflection staring back through broken shards, waiting for my tormentor to show me the damage I have caused. Firmly squeezing the sides of my marble sink, I embrace the pain caused by the tiny slivers of broken glass protruding from bloody knuckles, and prepare myself for whatever I am about to see. The first sequence of flashbacks shows me memories of finding my grandmother's chest, breaking in, and finding that wretched medallion.

Following memories I can recall, a bloody sea of new images begins tearing through my mind, increasing in speed the longer I stay in this unknown headspace. It isn't until the third set of images begins repeating itself that I recognize the pattern. These are the killings plastered all over the news, only sharing more detail and through the eyes of the killer. The close proximity to the slaughter victims increases exponentially. A first-person view of their severed flesh and decimated organs gliding in my hands. Blistering stomach acid shoots up my throat when the collection of images shows the victims' hearts being ingested.

"Stop!" I shriek, unsure of the connection this entity was trying to show me.

"Is something wrong? Did you not enjoy the memories of our time together?" Each word grates inside my head like nails on a chalkboard.

"I didn't kill those people!"

"Technically no, but also... yes. Your hand held the sharpened blade that annihilated those innocent women. It was your face

they saw before you ended their existence on this plane. Little fox, you are who the media is calling, 'The Butcher of Canadee'"

"That isn't possible! I would never hurt or kill anyone. I'm not a murderer."

Hysterical sobs escape me and before I know it, the bloody hands that cling to my tear-soaked cheeks leave trails of half-dried, deep mahogany stains.

"Whose blood is this?! Who did you make me kill?"

"Are you sure you want to know? I have been waiting impatiently for you to wake up to the destruction you have caused with your own bare hands."

"Tell me creature, whose blood is this?"

"A smaller prey than what I typically feast upon, but she smelled so good and tasted divine. Your best friend... Kyla James."

"You foul beast!" I scream, gut-wrenching sobs shaking my body. "How could you!?"

Leaving me without answers, I sense the abrupt disconnection of the parasitic leech attached inside me. All that lingers are the soft sounds of a distant maniacal cackle fleeting back to the depths of my psyche. My tormentor enjoys the anguish it's causing to not only me, but to the people around me. It has a motivation, a goal it wants to achieve and I'm the puppet for it to manipulate at its whim. Repulsed and overwhelmed from the events transpiring this morning, I throw on the shower tap as hot as it can go and step under the scalding stream, clothes and all.

With the weight of my actions too much to bear, I allow my body to slide down the previously cold tile and wrap my arms around my knees. Steam billows around my trembling frame. I watch in disgust as the water pouring down on me rapidly turns red the longer it soaks through my clothes. No amount of heat can provide comfort to my tissue as it suffers the consequences of my previously unknown actions.

As uneasiness washes over me, I close my eyes, lean my face up to the shower nozzle, and drift off under the bombardment of hot water. I am unsure what my next move is, but somehow I'll find the answers I need to solve this. I can't allow this entity to continue its massacre.

I need to stop it for good, even if that means I have to take myself down with it.

12

My body shivers under the once scalding water, breaking through the shocking morning revelation. Ice-cold water pelts my frame, freezing the fresh cuts and bruises on my body. Soaking wet clothes adhere to my skin, leaving goosebumps and near-colorless flesh behind, reminding me of the dead. Violent, bloody images play relentlessly in my mind, replaying memories I have no recollection of doing.

All women of similar size, shape, and appearance to myself running through the woods. Screams pierce painfully through my ears reflecting different nights of killing. Buckets of bright crimson saturate different sets of scrubs from work. Tear-soaked faces accompanied by pleas of mercy and justice. They just wanted to be let go and I didn't listen. I tore their flesh from their bones and licked it clean. My mental fortitude wasn't strong enough to fight through the paralyzed state of my brain to save them.

It was my hands that ripped their hearts out and feasted mercilessly on their flesh. Mothers, daughters, and sisters, were all taken from their lives due to this monster, and also because of me.

How could I kill my best friend? How was I capable of slaughtering five innocent women?

Stripping out of my drenched, red-stained clothes, I drop them at my feet with a squelching splat and warily make my way out of my bathtub. I feel numb, both physically and emotionally—a shell of the person I am. Ensanguined skin disfigures my reflection in the mirror. I can't stare long before I have to swallow my disgust and guilt back down my throat. Throwing up at this moment will fracture my last surviving thread of composure.

Dragging my feet across the bathroom tile and the carpet of my bedroom, I keep my head slumped down to avoid looking at the destruction in my bed. The devastating crush of guilt sinks further into me as I take each step toward my living room. I try to keep my thoughts neutral and attentive to my movements, despite the glaring reminder of my best friend's blood and flesh scattered across my bed linens, tugging at the last threads of my sanity. I want to burn them, I have to burn them.

Spotting a framed photo on the bookshelf featuring a teenaged version of Kyla and I wedges the dagger of remorse deeper into my splitting heart. Mourning cries break the silence in my apartment as I brace myself against the wall. She was the only person I had left who knew me better than I knew myself, and I murdered her in cold blood. Flashbacks of her desperate pleas for mercy repeat on a loop, fracturing me every time I hear her question, *"Rr-Rebakah? Is th-that you?*

How can you do this?" One paralyzing, three-letter word and I don't have the strength to answer—how?

Collapsing naked on the couch, sobbing under a blanket, I allow my thoughts to continue their downward spiral at the possibility of trying to explain this to someone. Do I go to the police? Where do I even begin? I don't want to hide what I've done, but whatever is consuming my mind needs to be stopped. I'm not a cold-blooded killer, I am someone who goes out of her way to save and protect others.

Reeling at the endless consequences of my actions, I make the mistake of turning on my living room television. Bold banners on the news channel throw more of my behavior in my face. Field journalists report outside the crime scene barrier that the serial killer has struck again. Panning over the crime scene, media coverage, and civilians fill the outskirts of the barrier. Jumbled conversations and shouting from many different angles. Outrage for what is happening to the victims and questions regarding the actions the local law enforcement is doing to keep this from happening again.

Clustered tightly behind the yellow tape, one reporter shouts in the direction of the police. "Sergeant Hamlin, do you have any suspects at this time?"

Ignoring the chaos, he throws up his hand to the camera and shouts, "No comment!" The hardened look of frustration is blatantly visible on the face of the newly appointed police Sergeant.

Hitting the power button on the remote and throwing it at the screen does little to alleviate the sorrow and hopelessness. There is no hope of escaping this new reality. The deafening silence is nearly too much, producing more heart-wrenching sobs in its place. The heaviness of my actions squeezes the inside of my skull and tugs my stomach further into knots. Grabbing the sides of my head, I scream a violent roar for it to stop. Lying crumpled in the fetal position on the couch, I recognize the familiar feeling that alerts me I am no longer alone.

"Do you not like what you have done little fox?"

Its voice cuts through the inner workings of my ears, clawing against the inside of the frayed edges of my mental capacity. "I didn't do it, you did!" Audible sobs flood harder from my broken composure.

"Au contraire. Remember, it was by your hand that these women have lost their lives, not I," the creature inside my mind roars back, a hint of amusement coating its words. Small vibrations pulse behind my eyes as he cackles wildly.

The next words to escape me come out restrained, absent of confidence, and pleading for answers. "What do you want with me? What do you gain from all of this?"

"Filthy human, I do not enjoy repeating myself!" Its scream reverberates in my skull.

"You want your Queen, I get that, but why am *I* part of the plan, and why is killing the only way to get her attention?"

"The more you kill, the more I get to see her return home to me. I am so close to ensnaring her in my web. The scarlet Queen is the ultimate prize and I have waited long enough to have her."

"I still don't understand what I have to do with this equation." Trying to wrap my head around his morbid and twisted game proves to be a mystery.

"You are testing my patience. I suggest you choose your next words wisely."

"Why is this so important? What is the secret you're not telling me?" I yell back louder, this time adding more sharpness to my words.

"After all these years, you let me out to play once more."

Taking a few deep steadying breaths, I close my eyes again to search through the kaleidoscope of repulsive imagery my parasite enjoys showing me. Sifting hastily through the goriest ones first, I try to latch onto a memory of significance. The muscles of my mind bend and stretch around old memories to bring forth when this monster took over my life. Within a couple of short minutes, a snippet from a few weeks ago flashes by. Stopping the images abruptly, I hone in on the last time I was at my grandmother's home... The day I sliced my hand and nearly bled out from arterial lacerations.

For the first time in weeks, a renewed sense of empowerment grows. A plot for revenge shakes the mental cobwebs loose, unfurling stealthily from its cage. My breaths quicken in excitement as adrenaline pulses through my core, restoring energy to my weak and atrophied tissues. I feel alive again. The corners of my mouth curl up in a devilish smile and a satiated sigh roots inside my throat.

I was thrust unwillingly into this vile game, but now it's my turn and I'm not one to play by the rules.

13

TWENTY-FIVE YEARS AGO

REMNANTS OF DECADENT, SEVERED FLESH AND EVISCERATED ORGANS encompass my every thought as I wander the shadowy boundaries trapping me in this wretched confinement. A disgusting cloak of mockery to my personalized haven, one last reminder of a former life bathed in blood—a time when I felt invincible.

Encased in the shadows of the night, I found pleasure in tearing through my victims' tissue with my bare hands. Now, I am reduced to replays of visceral screams escaping from faces drenched in pure terror and delicious last gurgles of my prey choking on their blood-filled final moments of air.

If only I could continue to feel the warmth of their blood on my skin and relive their lives draining from their trembling carcasses. Taste their life's essence as it slides effortlessly down my throat, staining my lips and teeth a remarkable shade of crimson. Thin, gaunt skin on my face rolls back over emaciated bones, exposing my sharpened incisors, curling into an unholy grin at the thought. Vivid recollections further disintegrate fragments of my sanity, but I welcome the slow drip of acid burning away the humanity that I once was.

My thirst for brutality was my downfall. Animalistic urges carelessly dragged me down the treacherous path that would inevitably lead to my capture. In spite of having already drained the life out of two women that evening, I simply could not stop. Driven mad by the insatiable need for more, I left my house and embraced the shadows of night without knowing it would be my last. Basking in the energizing glow from the full moon high in the sky, I barely made it two blocks up the road when my eyes caught sight of a spellbinding woman.

The first thing I noticed were the natural red, shoulder-length waves flowing around delicate facial features carved out of alabaster. Pouty lips stained a muted shade of pink paired with a subtle dusting of blush across round, freckled cheeks. There was a peacefulness to her aura and a sense of calm painted on her face and in her body language. Transfixed by her beauty, my mind contorted grim images of how exquisite her creamy white skin would look torn to shreds beneath my hands. She traversed the small streets of our quaint town unafraid and blissfully unaware of the cold-blooded killer walking amongst her.

Instead of luring my prey to my favorite wooded hunting grounds, I stayed patient and followed the copper-haired beauty back to her residence. She made it too easy for me by leaving the back door to the house unlocked. Leading directly into the kitchen, I silently snuck in through the sliding glass doors and promptly took notice of what lay in front of me on the counter.

Saliva pooled behind a wicked grin, as adrenaline coursed

through my veins in anticipation. I quickly grabbed the butcher knife from the block and tested the sharpness on the pad of my thumb. A sick satisfaction washed over me. Entranced by the light above the kitchen cabinets reflecting a hypnotizing, soft glow across the shining steel blade, I neglected a watchful eye on my prize.

High-pitched, ear-splitting screams accompanied by a glass breaking against the tile floor, severed the trance. Frozen in place, she threw her hands up in defense. "What do you want?" she squeaked out in fear.

Interwoven with desperation, I was unprepared for how melodious her voice would sound behind quivering lips. Refusing to give her the pleasure of a response, I stood there in silence, allowing the terror to gradually consume her.

She questioned again, only this time she tried and failed to add firm confidence to her words. "What do you want? Why are you in my house?"

Again, I did not grace her with a response. Engaged in locked eye contact, I stalked forward one step at a time in her direction, forcing her to back up into the corner section of the cabinets. Instantly, any trace amounts of bravery melted away under the physical force of my presence. Without taking her brown eyes off me, she frantically searched the countertop for something she could use to help her get away. Her breaths escaped faster and faster as the chances of her finding anything of use dwindled.

Taunting my prize further, I brought the knife up between us, breaking our lines of sight. I failed to hide the amusement in my voice when I sardonically asked, "Looking for this?"

Unblinking, wide eyes stared back in a fixed, haunted expression. I could not help but marvel at the way her skin drained of color under the crushing force of fear and panic.

To me, the best part of a kill is the build-up before death. Their delectable hearts pound ruthlessly in distress, igniting every predator trait rushing inside me. An addiction to the high their hopelessness feeds.

Quiet whimpers turned to heavy, pleading sobs. "Please! You don't have to do this. If you let me go, I won't tell anyone about this, I swear."

A thunderous roar of laughter belted from inside my abdomen at the absurdity of her request.

Tears streamed faster as her final words left her mouth. "Please God, help me."

"There is no god here sweetheart and if they were, they would not be helping you."

Away from the sound buffer of the pitch-black forestry, I plunged the knife into the left side of her neck, flawlessly slicing the carotid artery, and rendering her pleas for release incoherent. Only the handle was left exposed after the razor-sharp blade impaled precisely in place. For a split second, I watched the picturesque scene play out before me. Large amounts of blood gushed from the life-threatening wound, saturating her hair and blouse. Begging eyes screamed at me for help, while gasps for air choked on significant amounts of blood.

Instead of saving her, I leaned real close to her face, an unre-morseful grin on mine, and wrenched the knife from her neck, splattering the cabinets, floors, and walls in layers of crimson. Instinctively, my mouth found the fresh opening in her neck and darted my tongue out to play with the butchered pieces of flesh. Sweet, metallic, lifeblood poured down my awaiting mouth, sending the entirety of my body into an enraptured frenzy.

Incapable of waiting any longer, I gripped the blood-soaked knife in two hands above my head and stabbed it between the upper portion of her ribs. The unforgettable sound of bones snap-ping invoked unparalleled ecstasy. Shoving my hands inside the gaping wound, I used all of my strength to pry her chest cavity wide open. Muscle fibers stretched to their limits before shredding away from the bone and tearing out of the protective layers of flesh. Clinging to the very last seconds of her life, I took hold of her fighting heart and detached it crudely from her body. Her decimated corpse sat lifeless next to me on the kitchen floor while I fed savagely on her remains until my belly distended in fullness.

Annihilating her felt like my greatest accomplished masterpiece yet. Her cries of agony did not echo back from the preferred chase, however, the arterial spray painted across cream-colored walls and gray cabinets unlocked another dose of unexpected gratification. The vulnerability of being seen added another amplifying layer to the treacherous path that I carelessly walked. Relishing in her decimated beauty, my playtime was cut short because I was ambushed from behind. One surprise, powerful blow to the side of my skull sent me tumbling into unconsciousness.

Trapped in heavily rusted, metal chains against the cold, wet walls of a cellar, I was kept on the cusp of life and forced to watch my body's deterioration. My bowels were the first to fall victim to my harsh reality. The putrid stench of feces and urine saturated my clothes and ate away the layers of skin, leaving behind open, infected sores. My shoulder joints were next to collapse as athletic muscles painfully atrophied and dislocated from the sockets. Lack of hydration left behind fissures on my lips, tongue, and gums.

A small crack in the basement window displayed a fraction of the sun's rays, allowing me to count my days of suffering. Roughly seven days of denied food, water, or contact from the outside world. Alienated by my own hand, I knew the surviving members of my family would not come looking for me, or even notice that I had gone missing. Adjusting to prolonged exposure to damp, bone-chilling blackness, I began to welcome death in open, frail arms, but my capturer had other plans.

After a near immeasurable amount of time alone, an older, broad-shouldered man entered the cellar carrying an arsenal of devices at his side. With ease, he wordlessly unchained me from the wall and carried me over to a rusty examination chair similar to those found in an asylum. Bolted to the floor in the center of the room, its partially leaned back position exhibited three torn and stained cushions to orient patients in any manner. Both armrests had lost their padding, leaving broken pieces of corroded metal behind. Permeating over the horrid stench my body exuded, the contraption smelled of mildew and piss.

Holding me down with force, he secured my limbs, chest, and forehead in place utilizing the restraints attached underneath. Wide leather straps held my disintegrated body firmly giving me a slim chance of breaking free.

I could feel the tightness fracturing the small bones of my wrists and ankles. My frail body had no strength or motivation to fight my fate. Metal speculums were clamped onto my eyelids and widened to keep my eyes open to witness every action. Tiny rivulets of blood seeped down my face and eye sockets. Extending from behind the headrest, a circle gag made of metal attached to leather was shoved into my mouth between my teeth, forcing my jaw to unhinge from the joints. Cracking due to the pressure, my brittle back molars chipped away beneath the metal.

For the first time since he entered the cellar, my capturer broke the silence and started to whistle a merry tune of enjoyment.

Picking up a rusty pruning saw from the workbench, he shook it angrily in a clenched fist and stared down at me, a crazed look in his eyes. Utilizing his free hand, he held up an old, stained family photo in front of my face. Front and center sat a younger version of the exquisite meal I last feasted on. "I'm going to love how much this hurts you. You desecrated my grandbaby. An abhorrent, sadistic beast like you doesn't deserve to witness the sunrise any longer!"

Droplets of spit landed on my face and in my mouth as he spewed his words of hatred at me. Bound and gagged the way he wanted, there was little I could say or do that would change his mind.

Starting at the lower half of my body, he pinched the emaciated skin of my shin and painstakingly carved his way into me. The serrated edge of the saw callously tore away strips of withered flesh with lingering sinew from where it was attached to my bones. Constricted groans of my agony bellowed from behind the metal gag and blended in contrast to the squelching sounds of ripping flesh. Extreme malnourishment and dehydration prevented the full volume of my screams from being heard, but the satisfactory gaze from my executioner's face held everything I needed to see. He wanted me to bear witness and feel every slice, cut, and tear inflicted. Enjoyment and pride tugged at the outer corners of his mouth as he shoved the severed pieces down my open throat.

Strangled grunts of my suffocation were heard behind the indigestible amount filling my gaping mouth. My body's natural gag reflex tried to overcompensate and expel the contents out of my mouth, but firm hands blocked the opening, forcing me to choke on the bloody mass of tissue. I struggled violently against my restraints to no avail. Newly broken bones induced electrifying pain racing through my body. Noticing my quickened breaths from my nose, he slid one of his hands further up my face, blocking my last clutch to salvation. Too incapacitated to fight back, the loss of air from my lungs became a beacon of hope for my weakened state. An unworthy light guiding me down a path to my death.

I know I am undeserving of the mercy of being unable to recall the torturous events following what felt like my final breath, but I would rather be subjected to daily punishment instead of being sentenced to remain contained in this afterworld and forced to rot. No matter how hard my executioner tried to obliterate a sadistic beast, my thoughts forever revolved around my chosen prizes. Vile works of graphically artistic death created by me, and displayed for all to see, lived etched into the walls of my mind as each day blurred in that cellar.

Imprisoned for a second time, I now find myself sequestered in an alternate realm. Bewitched to match my favorite hunting grounds, I am trapped within the cage of what was, and no way of knowing what shall be.

Under a constant state of hovering darkness, all sense of day and time escapes the mind, further clawing away at lunacy. Opaque, dense layers of fog surround my legs but serve no purpose in impeding my stroll. Driven only by my murderous thoughts, my bearings of this realm prove no match to the maze of forestry stretched out before me and below me. Calloused skin on my bare feet ignore the jagged rocks and fallen branches gathered along my path. Carved-out areas from repeated lapses of pacing swerve around thick trunks of crumbling trees and underbrush. As far as my soul-less eyes can see, I am encompassed by dense rows of bare foliage and thorn bushes. A depressing palette of brown and gray, blank of the indescribable colors of life. The constant gnaw of unsatisfied hunger siphons from my mangled body but I stay beyond the earthly plane to experience a proper physical death.

Lost in the blackened, cavernous pits of my thoughts, a faint note of lavender blended seamlessly with a sweet, earthy aroma sneaks through the acrid scent of festering necrosis and destruction. Flaring my nostrils and expanding my decaying lungs to their limits, I allow the intoxicating scent to infiltrate my disintegrating mind. Euphoric bliss travels uninterrupted into my core and bridges the gaps in the fragments of destroyed tissue, electrifying impulses long since forgotten.

Whipping my head in the direction I believe the heavenly

fragrance has traveled from, I catch sight of a young girl traversing through my purgatory. Small amounts of hesitancy keep me cautious, yet intrigued, as I stay hidden amongst the shadows and under the concealment of the black cape draped over my unnatural form. Dressed in what appears to be cartoon pajamas, she clings her arms around the neck of a worn and tattered teddy bear. My unwavering gaze watches every movement of her head turning around in a panic, unaware of her surroundings.

As I make each soundless step toward my intruder, I realize that I am being driven by not only her exhilarating smell, but something I have craved with an unquenchable thirst—fear. The small stature of this human reeks of a smell so addicting, that I question if this is yet a trick of the mind or a tangible being sent to widen the gap between sanity and madness. I listen intently to the heavy thrums of her heart and watch as it visibly pulses under the soft pale skin of her neck. Perplexion further distorts my features at the startling addition to my impenetrable domain.

Children do not satisfy the carnal cravings driving my ruthless killings and yet, I am baffled by an unfathomable, gravitational pull this young creature has ensnared within me. The longer I endure staying entangled in the web of trickery, my eyes finally focus on a detail I have dangerously overlooked.

Smooth copper hair flows delicately in waves down the petite frame of her back, a near-perfect match to my victims, a wicked obsession I acquired long before adulthood. My feet move of their own volition closer to the mystery, expertly weaving to avoid being seen. Adding one step too many, I find myself close enough to reach out and tangle my monstrous fingers in her radiant hair. A strong vibration pulses around her and blocks my outstretched hand in potential warning. Words attempt to form, but before I can drag them from my dry, cracked throat, the captivating entity before me disappears, leaving no trace. Completely vanished in one blink, and yet her unforgettable presence still permeates the air all around me.

The smoldering fire left burning after my death comes roaring back to life, engulfing my core in eternal flames. The innocence of youth kept her from my grasp this time, but an indescribable awareness alerts me that this will not be the last time I am blessed with her visit. Uncoiling from the bottomless pit of my gut, a soft cackle starts to erupt into a deafening, diabolical howl.

Unbeknownst to her, she has just become my most desirable game yet.

I4

ONE DAY AGO CONTINUED

HELLBENT ON GETTING REVENGE AGAINST THE PARASITE WREAKING havoc on my life, I decide that now is the time for action. Bolting upright on my couch, I toss my blanket to the side with restored vigor. Ideas from all angles swarm my mind at a chance to be chosen. I can say with certainty that going to the police is not on this list. Ending the creature's game today and saving others holds all of my mind's attention and drive.

"Your plan is not going to work. Do you truly believe you can outsmart me?" it remarks suddenly.

Refusing to back down, my quick response holds no fear. "I don't have time for your shit right now, creature. Your battle for control over my body is a victory that you will not achieve. This ends today!"

Boisterous laughter echoes behind my eyes, a wordless response to my threat.

Realizing that I'm still naked from the shower, I hurriedly walk over to my laundry room for a new set of clean clothes and a trash bag for all of the bloody bed linens. I also snag an apron and a pair of gloves. In spite of the predicament I have precariously gotten myself in, I feel more alive in these moments than I have in weeks. This plan I have concocted is outlandish, though it seems to be the best way I can see any of this working out in my favor.

The hardest part of my plan so far is cleaning up my bedroom. It has been hours since I woke up wrapped in a comforter saturated in my best friend's blood and tissue. Looking at the bed now, I want to scream, cry, and give everything to rewind time to fight harder against my plagued mind.

"What an exquisite masterpiece you have made, little fox."

"She didn't deserve this!"

"The astonishment on her face when she saw that it was you who stood over her holding a knife. I can feast upon that image for centuries to come," the voice laughs in amusement.

"Stop it, stop it, stop it!" I shriek on the cusp of sobs.

Slowing down my breathing, I endeavor to ignore how fast my heart rate has accelerated and the sweat building on my forehead. This is all the parasites doing, not mine. Averting my eyes to the best of my ability, I start shoving my bed sheets in the trash bags. Fortunately, most of the blood has dried, or formed coagulated piles of sinew and flesh. It's taking all of my courage, strength, and willpower to do this without breaking down in tears or profusely vomiting.

Steadily bouncing my right leg distracts me enough to successfully remove the horror from my eyesight. I've cleaned up after traumas at work, however, staring at the destruction you caused to your best friend is far more impactful. Two heavy-duty trash bags later, my linens, towels, and clothes are all cleaned up. Leaving the hauled bags to the front door, I let out a breathy sigh and move forward with the plan

Glancing down at my counter near my front door, sitting neatly next to my cutting boards is my knife case. Cooking fresh meals is a life skill I take great pride in, mostly because my grandmother taught me that lesson. Knowing you can take a few simple ingredients and transform them into a savory, concoction for the tastebuds is unreal. Stuffing the case in my bookbag releases a quiet teardrop rolling down my cheek. I know this won't be easy by any means, so I stifle the brewing sadness and push forward.

Sitting down on my couch, I open up my coffee table cabinets to reveal my grandmother's special stationery box. Completing this section of my mission is incredibly bitter-sweet and in some odd way therapeutic all by itself. Writing this note is vitally important, therefore I won't stay here longer than is necessary. Visceral memories of the massacres I have created, and flashbacks of the undisclosed reaffirm the actions driving me forward now.

Dabbing the tear-soaked corners of my eyes, I take a lap around my apartment, entranced by the storm of happy stories that transpired here. Late-night movie sessions with Kyla, small get-togethers surrounded by amazing coworkers, and the unique ways we change and grow over the years. Reminiscing of all the hours that Kyla and I spent together inside these walls, brings another rush of tears to my eyes. I knew that picturing her smiling face again would break the dam holding me together. Grasping my head around the fact that my best friend watched me destroy her from the inside out is a tough thing to digest.

Loading everything in my arms, I lock the door to my apartment and don't even bother to glance back as I head outside. Shoving the bags in the Jeep, I drive off in the direction of my next task.

The day the paramedics carried me out was the last time I stepped inside my grandmother's house. Ignoring the rest of the home, I make my way directly up to the attic. I know I'm prepared enough for the devastation waiting for me to find. Slamming the door open a few weeks ago has left it slanted and hanging crooked on the hinges. Pushing it lets out an eerie creak, revealing the substantial, dried, viscous stain of dark brown blood. Expanding my lungs to capacity and controlling my breathing allows me to take in the gory scene in stride. This is not the time to allow for panic and anxiety to sink their claws.

The paramedics arrived shortly after I had already passed out from extensive blood loss. I thought I was dead and a small part of me wished for death to take me that day. I gradually began to accept my fate, only to awaken hours later in the hospital, connected to tubes and heart monitors. That moment in time no longer controls the outcome of today.

Lying next to the bloody outline of where my body collapsed, is the golden nightmare I believe started this whole thing. Huffing in annoyance, I blow a kiss to my grandmother's rocking chair, snatch the object off the wooden floor, and head downstairs in the direction of the backyard.

A few feet away from the back porch, in the center of our backyard sits the fire pit that my family built when I was younger. Approximately six feet in diameter, the outer circle of stones is made up of thick river rocks and secured smaller stones that my family helped me gather from this very yard.

Dragging the stuffed trash bags from my Jeep to the pit,

the sun begins to set, so I don't have a lot of time to burn this before nightfall. Living at the end of the street doesn't always mean total privacy. Neighbors can be nosey and loathsome.

Limited in my time, I place the trash bags directly in the middle of the fire pit, slice open the top using one of my knives, and douse the contents in lighter fluid. A flick of a match and everything engulfs in flames instantly. The gentle, evening breeze provides a rush of energy for the fire. Blazing heat from the flames nearly burns the skin on my exposed arms. Unaware that burning dried blood gives off an odor, the acrid stench of death permeates the air around me, causing dry, stinging coughs.

Miraculously, the flames don't grow too high to be seen, although the black-tinted, demonic smoke rising above may cause a few disturbances. Assuming my linens have fully burnt, I loop back around the side of the house, letting the fire continue to consume on its own. I say a soft 'see you soon' and leave my grandmother's place.

Driving to my final destination on this trip is immensely difficult. Numerous racing thoughts cross my mind, blurring the lines of comprehension. I know for certain that what I'm doing is irrational and won't make it appear logical to anyone, thus I have faith in myself that there is a chaotic method to my madness.

Finally arriving at the state park, the last few rays of sun glow over the gated entrance, casting a rich blend of purple, pink, and orange across the sky. The warmth from the day lingers as the chilliness of night rolls in. One last look at the sunset is all I need to carry on and move forward. Lugging my bookbag out of the Jeep, I lock my doors and refuse to look back as I cross the barricaded entrance to the hiking trail.

The further down the path I walk, the swirling emotions

conflict and reassure me at the same time. I pause every few feet to balance my breathing and ground myself to the earth beneath my feet.

The forest air around me buzzes in anticipation, circling me in their own version of a welcome. We often forget that the forest and the nature that always surrounds us are alive. It moves and bends with us, we just need it to allow it to be there for us. Being out in the woods makes me feel complete and whole. A place where I belong.

Not too far down the gravel pathway, my feet stop abruptly. Minimal light shines through the woods, and yet, I am awestruck at the most gorgeous, breathtaking, red maple tree I've had the pleasure of seeing in person. Slivers of light feature stunning shades of claret leaves and thick, sturdy boughs. The exposed, interwoven roots growing up to the impressive trunk, blending seamlessly out to the smaller branches peppered with leaves, could be a perfect match to the one I used to sit under at my grandmother's house. This is where I am supposed to be this evening. The closer I get to the base of the tree, the stronger my mind and body feel. My breaths even out, lucidity comes to my mind, and the incomprehensible anxiety melts away.

Thick, clusters of tree leaves don't hold space for the stars in the night sky above the forest to shine their gleaming light down upon me, and yet, I know they are there. I've always felt my family's protective eyes looking out for me.

Intuitively knowing that the time is right, I unzip my bookbag and slide the boning knife out of the case. Bracing my back against the sturdiest part of the trunk, I place the gold medallion in my left hand and grasp the knife in my right. Touching the tip of the knife in the middle of my left palm, directly in line with the medallion, I precisely carve the blade slowly up the inner forearm and finish in my elbow ditch.

The burning and stinging sets in immediately as the waterfall of blood drenches my arm and lap. Counteracting the intrusion, my body's natural endorphin response reacts instantaneously. Similar to high doses of morphine, my mind and body feel weightless until it settles and crashes me back down to reality.

For years, I've told my patients that if you look away, the pain isn't as bad. Unfortunately, due to the amount of damage caused, I can truthfully say that is an astronomical lie. The pain is excruciating and incomprehensible. Seconds have passed and my arm is violently numb, cold, and almost impossible to move. Unwavering beats of my heart pulse throughout my entire body. Short, heightened, breaths pant out of my mouth.

Firmly clutched in my hand, the gold medallion is drenched in blood. This stupid antique has done nothing except destroy my life and all of the people close to me. Severing muscles, multiple major arteries, and vital anatomical structures, annihilates all chances of being rescued. I am now unshackled from the burden that has destroyed my life.

If I had known the outcome of the day ahead of time, I would have happily died in the attic. With me gone, it gives women a chance for survival, another day for success.

Counting my last languid, deliberate breaths, the minutes of self-inflicted agony tick by slowly. Faintly, I hear a hollow shout break my thoughts. *"You insufferable wench! What have you done?"*

The word escapes my mouth with absolutely no hesitation. "Check."

15

Blaring at max volume, the incessant beeping of my alarm clock grinds against my eardrums. Throwing my arm out towards my nightstand, I direct a solid smack to the top, shutting it off instantly. *Fuck!* Acute pain bolts across my sutured palm, sending a shock of nerve spasms up my arm. Dazed from the jarring alarm, I thoroughly forgot about my wounded hand. Laying motionless diagonally across the bed, I close my eyes until the throbbing subsides.

Drastically changing the sound volume in the room, the deafening silence isn't any better than the dissonant alarm.

Chaos from my nightmare spins wildly behind my eyes. I'm stuck in this endless loop of vulnerability, sinking further in a trap and having no way of escaping. Hell-bent on carnage and pinned mercilessly in a savage cage.

I don't know how to be vulnerable. My entire life has been about survival, not living. Now I am left exposed raw, helpless, and subjected to an insidious game of cat-and-mouse. Burning under a magnifying glass, and scrutinized by everyone for failing to provide the answers they desperately need. The blinding truth that I can't solve everything by myself is unavoidable and yet, my self-sabotaging behavior suggests otherwise.

The question of who is targeting me and who was screaming for me to wake up chants like a broken record in the forefront of my mind. The ominous, macabre forest deathscape persistently plagues me, however, this is the first time I've heard that rough, masculine voice.

For my entire life, my nightmares have never been this surreal, nor has anyone ever spoken to me, in any facet of the illusions—until now. Its taunting tone reveled in the tortured screams rupturing from my throat. I am at a loss trying to comprehend what the voice meant by saying it's been watching me for eons. What does that even supposed to mean, and how am I supposed to figure something out when I am devoid of a logical explanation for the events that have transpired recently? This whole situation has left me immensely frustrated that my analytical mind is having diffi-culty comprehending this unnaturally occurring phenomenon.

As much as I would love to stay in bed all day, avoid my responsibilities, and critically break down this situation, in the end, I have a job that requires my attendance. Doing my best to avoid crushing my hand, I cautiously try rolling on my side. Mid-turn, a stabbing pain squeezes my leg, nearly doubling me in half. Reaching under the covers, palpable heat radiates outward from my right calf. Yanking the covers off and glancing down, I immediately see the cause of my distress.

Covering the entirety of my lower leg, including the knee, are unidentifiable, irregular vein markings and discolorations of blackened, purple bruising. Inflammation of the tissue has already settled in, visibly indicating extensive injury. When I went to bed last night, aside from my hand, the rest of my body was sore and exhausted, not physically injured. Rewinding the past week in my head, I'm unable to pinpoint an isolated incident where an injury causing this much damage has taken place. Thinking of the vivid illusion of last night's horrific dream sends a haunting shiver along my skin.

Palpating the flesh, it's hot to the touch and exceptionally tender. Testing my mobility of the leg, I can wiggle my toes at the same time as rolling my ankle, proving to be no issue. Moving my foot along the sheet to bend at the knee, dispatches another round of burning pain up my leg. Nothing appears to be broken, however this self-tested prognosis is inconclusive.

Using all of my willpower, I inch my way across the sheets and out of bed. It takes a few tries to catch my breath, and then I am semi-upright and off my mattress. Bracing myself alongside the wall, I stand in one spot to gather my bearings and ease a spell of vertigo. The room around me momentarily tilts horizontally back and forth. Hobbling on the outside of my bad leg, I shift all of my weight to my non-dominant, potentially steady leg. Using the wall for leverage, I look rather ridiculous bunny-hopping my way to the kitchen freezer for ice. The look on Jack's face right now would be priceless. I can picture him now, leaning against the arm of my couch, phone in hand, recording me in all of my hard-headed glory.

Roughly halfway there, my stable leg gets caught on a pile of clothes haphazardly in the middle of my cluttered walkway. It took a fraction of a second for me to face plant onto the floor. Thank goodness for the carpet, or I would have more than the two wounds I've collected. Coincidentally, that pile of clothing is from last night. The same pile of work clothes that I couldn't be bothered to put in the hamper. If I believed in karma, I would say that she is a bitch, and got me back for being lazy. Boy, I am glad Jack isn't here to witness this.

Although placing pressure on the disfigured leg is difficult, I am too damn stubborn to call anyone for help. Rejecting assistance means I need to be resourceful, and since I am currently on the floor, my only option is to tuck my prideful tail between my legs and crawl.

Awkwardly scooting on my butt, and using one arm to pull myself further along the tile floor, I eventually reach my freezer. A quick thank you to past me for getting a refrigerator with a freezer drawer on the bottom, and I am ready to continue. An ice pack in hand, I shimmy my way back across the length of my kitchen and to my work duffle left by the front door. In addition to the ice, I collect a compression wrap from my bag and clumsily head toward my couch.

Completely out of breath and covered in sweat from the unexpected workout, I surrender my aching body to the extra soft cushions. What my pride didn't account for when avoiding assistance, is the fact that now my entire body hurts worse than it did when I went to bed—including the unexplained injury to my leg. Black dots distort my vision and a sudden adrenaline rush to my head disorientates my bearings. Steady heartbeats pulse heavily down my neck and throughout my limbs. Grounding my breathing using slow, methodical counts, my ravenously hungry, rumbling stomach perforates the sounds of my exhalations. Staring at the distance from the couch to the counter, I instantly regret not grabbing a snack while in the kitchen. Tough shit to my stomach because now it needs to be patient and wait until I feel motivated to crawl again.

Reaching for my vibrating cell phone on my coffee table, the screen unlocks to a packed notification bar of multiple missed calls and countless text messages from Jack. Placing my phone on silent while a homicidal maniac is on a spree-killing streak wasn't the best move on my part, and certainly not my brightest of ideas.

Knowledgeable enough to avoid his text messages to call him instead, I hit his number on speed dial and unenthusiastically wait for the lecture about my safety.

It didn't make it to the second ring when Jack's smart-mouthed voice clicks in my ear. "Well, it's about time you picked up your phone. Were you planning on sleeping the entire day?"

I want to tell him that I woke up to an alarm and wasn't sleeping the day away, although biting my tongue is the smarter option. "Look, I'm terribly sorry. I had it on silent because I desperately needed sleep," I reply defensively. I am not one to give out apologies lightly, especially anyone who isn't Jack, however, behind my apathetic inflection, I do sincerely mean my apology.

"Last I checked, I distinctly told you to keep your sound on," he scolds, a low growl of frustration escapes his throat. An action I do not believe he meant for me to hear.

"Yes. Yes, I know. What is so important that you had to spam my phone with notifications?"

"I've been at the station all morning. I was calling to let you know about some of the evidence the police have found out about our latest victim, Rebekah."

My ears perk up at the mention of her name. "I just got up not too long ago and haven't left my house. Do you want me to wait for you here or meet you at the morgue?" I question, failing to hide the excitement in my voice.

"Meet me at the morgue. I'll get coffee on the way."

"You're the best, Jack"

"Tell me something I don't know," he replies, quickly ending the call absent a goodbye.

Forgetting momentarily about my injured limb, I pause when a sudden twist of my torso, triggers unhindered spasms down my spine, wraps around the front of the injured leg, and stops in my toes. Stuck halfway between sitting up and leaning against the cushions, I deliberately reposition myself to an elevated orientation rather than snuggling warmly under a blanket for the rest of the day. A couple of calculated breaths later and I can bend forward without pain.

Despite sitting here for a meager ten minutes, I am pleasantly gobsmacked when I pull off the ice pack. Previously inflamed, marred skin is replaced by a normal-sized calf, healed bruising, and only little patches of faint erythema remain. Scrutinizing my legs' appearance, I am well and truly perplexed. The palpable heat and the throbbing in the knee joint has vanished as well. This morning, I could hardly walk, and now it doesn't even look injured.

Convinced my eyes are playing a nefarious trick on me, I briskly rub them against my knuckles and blink rapidly for a few seconds. Refocusing my now blurry vision, an injured leg is not what I see propped up on the pillow in front of me.

Considering Jack is probably waiting for me and wondering what's taking so long, I shake my head a few times and stuff my baffling morning in a locked mental box to tackle later. Despite my leg looking and feeling better, I decide to wear the compression bandage, erring on the side of caution.

"You will not escape me again."

Darting my attention upward and away from my leg, I swivel my head back and forth in search of the scarcely audible hoarse voice. Failing to hear any questionable sounds, I recklessly suspect no one is in the room with me. A sharp look at my front door confirms my suspicions since the deadbolt and door chain are secured in place.

Similar to the undetectable visitor last night, the words croaked out gravelly and distorted, muddled in their delivery. Letting the silence fill the space in my living room, I listen closely for the voice to return.

No sound reverberates back to me.

Restarting the compression wrap around my leg, I manage to loop the roll one time, and without warning, the bundle abruptly drops from my stiff fingers. I am immobilized and rigid in place. The unearthly cloak of eeriness engulfs my mind and the atmosphere around me. Uneasiness and panic violently rip their way inside me, replicating the hellish aura from my nightmares. I am being forced to relive the darkest, cavernous pits of fear during the day. What haunts me behind closed eyes found its way to me.

Paralyzing, high-pitched scratching pierces against the inner walls of my skull, distorting my face in anguish. Increasing in both volume and frequency, the grating continues longer than I can articulate. Clasping my hands around my ears does nothing to relieve the spine-chilling agony. Vanishing instantaneously, a voice takes its place.

"Do I have your attention now, my Queen?"

Amplified by the small cavity, my tormentor's words echo clearly in my mind.

"Leave me alone!" I shout.

"And miss witnessing you crumble? I think not, my sweet," the voice taunts inside my head.

"What do you want with me?" I yell back.

Sinister cackles rattle between my ears.

Huffing in annoyance, I snatch my belongings from the coffee table and storm off toward my bedroom. Scattered, incomprehensible scenarios jumble internally. This can't be happening right now. There is an answer, I just need to figure out what it is, and then this will all disappear.

"I have already explained this. You are mine and I will not be allowing you to escape my clutches again. Do I. Make myself. Clear?"

"You are a breakdown of the functionality of my brain due to lack of sleep, high amounts of unmanaged stress, and an acute hemorrhaging laceration. Insomnia induced. Active psychosis," I spit out the last words from gritted teeth.

"I knew from the first moment I saw you, that this game between us would be most satisfying." An ear-splitting roar lingers after its words disappear.

Wrenching a pillow off my bed, I shove it against my face and let out the loudest, unrestrained scream my lungs can muster. Heavy pants briskly morph into unbridled sobs.

Shuffling my way toward the bathroom, endless tears waterfall down my cheeks, mingling with snot pouring out my nose. The gravity of everything I am experiencing has finally caught up to me. I feel as if my body and mind are breaking in half.

Wiping my face on a clean washcloth, I repeat, *this is temporary,* ad nauseam to the reflection in the mirror. Coming to terms that I can't tackle this on my own, I reach for the cabinet containing my anxiety medication. I avoid them for clarity of mind, except my mind is anything other than clear at this time. Taking medication does not make me weak, it simply means I need a little assistance and I am not alone. Swallowing down the tiny blue pill dispatches a cloak of serenity over me. *This is temporary.*

Stepping back in my room, the glow of my clock resting on my nightstand reminds me I am going to be late meeting Jack. Grabbing the work clothes on top of the dresser, I throw them on, brush my teeth, and plop my hair up in a bun. Knowing my work bag is all ready to go, I gather my keys, and I am on my way.

16

DRIVING AROUND THE BACKSIDE OF THE MORGUE, I PARK MY BLACK Chevy Traverse habitually in the spot to the right of Jack's 4Runner. Our timing couldn't be more impeccable because as soon as I shut off the engine, I catch sight of Jack walking around the front of his vehicle. Balanced neatly in his arms is a large box labeled Evidence and a brown drink tray containing coffee from our favorite local cafe.

Gulping down a few steadying breaths, I grab hold of my work bag and step out.

"Well, don't you look rough this morning," Jack jokingly teases.

Barely holding myself together from this morning's *activity*, I ignore his comment and walk around him to the double doors. I would like to tell him everything that is going on because I know he will understand, it just has to wait until we figure out more of this case.

Walking inside, Jack wastes no time slamming the evidence box on an examination table, alongside the drink tray. Tossing the top off, he quietly pulls out an assortment of clear evidence bags.

"Are you going to tell me what this is about?" I ask after a couple moments of silence.

"I got an urgent call from Sergeant Hamlin requesting my appearance at the station. He mentioned it was important and my presence was needed quickly. I tried texting you and got no response. After he told me what was going on, that was when I started calling you and still got no response," he replies, a hint of annoyance behind his calm words.

Masking the crack in my voice, I make an effort to settle the tension between us and steer the conversation in a different direction. "Can we not do this right now? My day hasn't started out well and I've already apologized, forgive me. What did you find out?"

"For starters, I accept your apology, I'm giving you a hard time." Holding up his index finger at me, he gulps down some of his coffee before finishing his reply. "When the cops went to investigate Rebekah's apartment, they discovered a handful of questionable things."

"Questionable how?" I ask, quirking my eyebrows and canting my head in curiosity.

"The officers were shocked to see that her apartment was kept organized and clean. No signs of struggle or forced entry. However, they did find a bloody pillowcase in the hallway close to her bedroom."

Pulling a large bag out of the evidence pile on the table, a pale green bloody pillowcase is bundled at the bottom.

"Exquisite."

Startled by the unexplainable voice in my head, without warning, I grip the edge of the table using my left hand to stabilize myself. An exceedingly poor way to hide being momentarily disarmed by an unseen disturbance.

Reaching over the table, Jack gently places his hand over mine and asks in concern, "Ray, you okay?"

"Yeah, I'm fine." Rubbing the back of my other hand to conceal the fresh beads of sweat forming on my forehead, I avoid telling him the truth and carry on with our conversation. "A bloody pillowcase? That doesn't correlate with how we found her. There was too much blood at the crime scene for it to be hers, and according to the pre-examination report, she only had the forearm laceration."

"Exactly, they don't believe it is hers," he replies, a look of worry for me still carved in his features.

"Not trying to be inconsiderate here, but that doesn't justify immense urgency, what was so important that you spammed my phone?" My words snap out more disrespectful than I intended.

"While they were searching her apartment and digging deeper into her background, they figured out a lot of critical pieces to the puzzle. The first being that a few months ago, she inherited her grandmother's house," he says, leaving room at the end of his statement, and preparing for me to ask the inevitable follow-up.

"What is so important about her grandmother's house?" I question in a sarcastic, playful tone, bobbing my head side to side.

"So glad you asked!" he chuckles theatrically. "There were plenty of secrets hidden inside the walls of that house, some of which I don't believe Rebekah knew about. The cops are still going through everything."

"Jack... Get to your point."

"When Rebekah was a little girl, her mother was brutally murdered in that home. According to police records, it was her grandfather, Cole Musing, who found her decimated corpse that same evening."

"Did they ever catch the person who did it?" I ask. Excitement and curiosity spiking my heart rate.

Seeing the enthralling interest written in my facial features, Jack's tone lightens up and carries traces of elation. "Turns out, her grandfather caught the killer eating her organs on the kitchen floor."

"Hold on," I pause, temporarily trying to summon where I heard a familiar tale, "I faintly remember this story, wasn't it plastered all over the news?"

Unprepared for what awaited me next, Jack pulls another bag from the pile in front of us. Inside is the clipping of the front page from the local paper dated twenty-five years ago. Featured front and center is a picture of police officers escorting a tall, rugged man outside of a grand, picturesque home in handcuffs. Behind them in the back of the frame is what appears to be an older woman clutching a young girl to her chest, averting her eyes from witnessing the traumatic event. The caption underneath reads, "Pictured above: Canadee Police arrest a local man after investigating the report of a dead body found in the resident's home."

Engulfed by the article, I'm startled when Jack proceeds to fill me in on the rest of the details. "That," he points to the newspaper still firmly in my grasp, "is where it begins to get interesting. The grandfather never called the police. He starved and tortured that man for weeks and was only discovered after a neighbor saw his mangled corpse through a crack in the cellar window."

"Bastard thought he could break me."

Shifting my body against the table, I close my eyes and

kneed a soft knuckle clockwise around my temple. I thought the medication would make the gravelly voice disappear, not manufacture distracting comments about the situation happening in front of me. My top priority is to concentrate on Jack and keep all of the facts straight.

"*Go away!*" I yell at the voice telepathically.

Noticing my lack of response accompanied by my odd behavior, Jack carries on, filling me in on the rest of the story. "Obtaining the search warrant, police uncovered the grandfather's torture lair in the cellar. The smell alone caused seasoned veteran officers to vomit uncontrollably. Hanging upside down on one of the walls via chains, was the mangled, decaying corpse of an unidentifiable man. A fifty-five-gallon drum barrel sat below him containing copious amounts of rotting flesh, and eviscerated organs soaking in gelatinous blood. Sizeable chunks of his body had been skinned and based on how much blood was found at the scene, investigators concluded he was alive when it took place. They also speculated that Cole was attempting to perform some type of demonic ritual with blood, but never pursued that line of theory."

Comparing that scene to the violent ones I have been called to, no wonder those officers had a hard time containing their stomachs. "*Hmm*, that form of display strikes rather specifically. Did the Musing family report the granddaughter's murder to the police after capturing the killer?"

"It's documented that the grandmother is the one who made the call, however, it is written that the detective at the time never interviewed the grandfather." Pulling out another bag containing newspaper clippings pertaining to another case, he continues, "The horribly terrifying twist, is that the victim wasn't truly a victim. Turns out, he was later identified via a DNA match in CODIS as the suspect in a string of murders, and had a serious compulsion for women with a pale complexion and red hair, just like our current butcher."

Flashes of our unsolved crime scenes displaying disemboweled women hung from the forest trees invokes an unsettling feeling deep inside my core. "Are we looking at a copycat? Has anyone checked to see if the grandfather is still in jail? Have the police interviewed him?"

"Police tried, but when they arrived at the prison, the correctional officers discovered he hung himself using his bed sheets. They claimed he has been a model prisoner and showed no signs of suicidal ideation when evaluated."

Thoughts twist and contort in my mind, displaying fragments of varying degrees. "What are the odds that two people in the same family commit suicide so close together? Did the family have any contact in jail?" I ask curiously.

"They are looking over the prison logs, however, they haven't obtained any record of contact between him and the family. After Cole Musing confessed to the murder, the grandmother continued to raise Rebekah in that house until she moved out and settled in her apartment. Apparently, after the investigation, all entrances to the cellar have been sealed shut. The grandmother, Amelia, died from a heart attack a few months ago."

"Amelia must have known about Cole's private, late-night activities then," I quip. It's rude to speak ill of the deceased and yet, a chuckle manages to squeak beyond my lips.

Jack's eyes dart to meet mine, a silent question wondering what is so funny. Struggling to maintain my composure, I let out a trickle of inappropriate giggles and shrug back in response.

"Since all involved parties are deceased, they've centered

their investigation on Rebekah. Further diving into her life, Officer Penelope Ren revealed a vital incident that occurred a few weeks ago. Rebekah needed life-saving measures for, get this," Jack hesitates, intentionally making me wait, "arterial lacerations of her palm by an unidentifiable object."

My jaw drops wide enough to catch flies. "Wait, what? How did she discover this information?" I probe in astonishment. Anticipatory buzzing lights up my skin that I may have a link to the abnormal events eclipsing my life.

"Oh, now you're interested in what I have to say," he accuses light-heartedly, crossing his arms in front of his chest.

"Here's the thing," *smack*, "you're going to tell me," *smack*, "the rest of the information," *smack*.

Swatting my hand away from lightly tapping his arm, a wide smile forms on his face displaying two perfect dimples. "Tell me again why I put up with you?" he laughs infectiously.

Smack "We've been in each other's lives way too long, you're stuck with me now."

"Wouldn't have it any other way," he remarks, before returning to the story. "Rebekah was an ER nurse at Canadee Memorial. She called EMS after accidentally cutting her palm. Fortunately, paramedics got there in the knick of time because she nearly hemorrhaged out upstairs in the attic, practically amputating all of her fingers on her left hand. Coworkers barely saw her after that. They did mention that when she returned to work following mandatory leave, she was behaving strangely."

"Behaving strangely how?" I question impatiently.

"Easily distracted, talking to herself, and avoiding others," Jack reads from a small notebook in his hand.

"Anything else?"

"Uhh yeah, there is also this. Detectives found it in Rebakah's apartment," Jack says, hesitantly handing me an evidence bag containing what appears to be a folded letter with my name written on the front.

Drawing the oversized, mounted rotation light closer to the autopsy table, I slide on a pair of gloves to retrieve the envelope. Unfolding it meticulously, a breath catches in my throat at the words written.

Destroy it.
Do not let Ondrayus win.

17

SEVEN WORDS.

The burdening load held by two small sentences paralyzes my whole body instantaneously. A hollowness forms in my gut and the quickened, thrumming beats from my heart fill the entirety of available space in my throat; seizing any words from escaping. Choked silently by a letter that naturally gives the impression of simplicity, not the underlying message meant discreetly for me. Everything clicks solidly in place and crumbles simultaneously around me.

Is this why this case, and more specifically, this unsub has affected me drastically? How did Rebekah know?

Snapping his fingers in front of my face to pull me from the trance the letter placed me in, Jack's voice breaks the hold. "Earth to Ray, you in there?"

Blinking wildly, I manage to stutter out a handful of words. "I-I have to go... now."

"Wait, what do you mean you have to go?"

Snatching the evidence bag containing the gold medallion off the table, I bolt in the direction of the double doors leading out of the morgue. Jack's long arms manage to form a soft hold on my elbow, except the momentum from my long legs untethers us sooner than he hoped.

Running out to my vehicle, my words ring throughout the parking lot. "Let me go, Jack, this isn't your fight!"

He refuses to listen and pushes after me. "What is happening? You never keep things from me. What was on that note?"

I barely make it to my car when Jack firmly takes hold of the door frame, preventing me from closing it.

Up to this point, I've avoided making eye contact with him. I couldn't bear to witness the extinguishing of my best friend's flame. The devastation plaguing his facial features shatters my core. Overwhelming sobs break me from the inside out. "Please, you don't understand."

"Then help me understand damn it!" he cries, agony bleeding in his words.

Putting my Traverse in drive, I stomp on the gas and floor it out of the parking lot, narrowly missing Jack's body.

Refusing to look back in the direction of the individual who means the world to me, I keep my tear-streaked eyes locked on the road. Horns blare at my lunacy treacherously weaving between cars and ignoring red lights at top speed. My body burns turbulently.

"Fear not my sweet, I will take great care of you."

"I have escaped your clutches my entire life, you stand no chance."

"How naive you are to think of us as an equal match."

Screeching my tires in an out-of-control, pedal to the floor stop, my apartment dumpster and SUV almost collide violently together. Yanking the keys from the ignition, I sprint straight to the complex side entrance and scramble my way upstairs to my apartment.

Once inside, I slam the door behind me and click all of the hard locks in place, securing me and my hostile parasite alone. Bracing my back against the door, I look around the space in front of me. It's hard to believe that this morning I woke to such torment and pain. Now a renewed vigor nestles in my bones. The trick of the mind and skillful manipulation of my body rains clear behind my eyes. I don't know how I didn't see it earlier. Unsure how to end this vile plague, an unbalanced, deranged plan sets me on the path to my bathroom.

Aggressively smashing open the mirrored cabinet, glass shatters at my feet, leaving minor cuts on my hands and gashes down the exposed skin of my legs. Stinging erupts along my flesh and droplets of vibrant blood splatter to the floor. Searching the broken cabinet and sink basin for two specific orange bottles, I leave smears of blood on multiple surfaces and miscellaneous unopened medical supplies. Relief floods my chest cavity when I find the prescription bottles, releasing deep breaths out of tightened lungs.

Sweaty, blood-covered hands hectically fail to remove the caps. Breaking the child protection lock, I open my hand and pour excess amounts of sleeping pills and anxiety medication out of each bottle. Indecision guides my feet mindlessly back and forth across the carpet. Sweat glistens on my forehead and pale skin flushes due to exertion. Heightened senses make me keenly aware of the precarious and vulnerable situation that this could leave me in. Bellows of rage permeate all corners of my apartment. Accelerated heartbeats pulse in my throat, sending rounds of burning stomach acid up my esophagus.

This decision can not be made in haste, and yet, there is no time left to prepare.

"You already know the answer and how to find me."

"It's a trap! You're not real!" I shout fearlessly.

"I can assure you that I am indeed real, you know this to be true."

Uncurling my gauze-covered, sutured palm, a mixture of blue pills coated in blood stares back at me waiting for the selfish decision to be taken. Furious pounding on my front door halts my hand midway to my mouth, preventing me from gulping down a wicked concoction.

"Rayna, please, open up!" Jack calls between hard bangs. "I can't let you do this alone!"

"Pity."

Uncomfortable silence fills the charged air around me, leaving prickles of electrifying caresses on my skin. In one breath, I shove the handful of pills in my mouth and gag until their chalky coating and metallic taste leaves my throat. The uncomfortable wait begins.

Retrieving the medallion from my pocket, I protect it defiantly in my free hand. "I refuse to allow you to witness this. Let me fight this battle alone," I shout at the now silent door.

Foolishly believing Jack left, chaos erupts seconds after my words yell out. Bouldering all of his 6'3" frame into my apartment door, it smashes free from the locks and splinters the wooden frame.

Standing firm in front of me, his chest heaves in a desperate search for air. His red, swollen eyes search my distressed, bloody flesh up and down, stopping when he sees the empty bottles at my feet.

"What did you do?" he chokes out behind new tears.

"This is the only way for me to defeat him. I have to go to him," I mutter out.

In three quick strides, he's standing directly in front me. Gripping the outsides of my arms, he shakes me, searching my face for answers. "Defeat who?" he pleads, "you're not making any sense."

Glancing over at the clock, it hits me how long I have been staring at Jack's distraught face covered in unhindered tears waterfalling down his cheeks.

"I don't have much time to explain."

"Try... please," he begs.

Jack

PLEADING FOR ANSWERS, RAY'S BODY COLLAPSES LIMPLY AGAINST MY chest. Securing an arm under her knees, and one cradling her back, I walk her over-medicated body to the bedroom to tuck her in. Checking her pulse, it remains strong and consistent. I'm helplessly scared and exceedingly confused.

Softly running the side of my thumb across her cheek, heavy-lidded eyes flutter closed. "Jack," she says quietly, absent of the strength her voice regularly carries.

Ray manages to mutter out my name and it rips my chest to shreds, eliciting more tears to fall. Squeezing her hand, I place a gentle kiss on her knuckles. "I'm right here."

Catching a lone tear on her cheek, her eyes open and find mine. Vulnerability. That's what I see when her mesmerizing dark brown eyes with flecks of amber catch mine. Fear and panic saturate the air between us.

"When I was a little girl," she coughs, "I saw my father shove my mother down the stairs to her death."

"Shh, it's alright." Stroking the sweaty hair out of her face, I regain miniscule amounts of composure. We've experienced countless trials and tribulations over the course of our lifetime together, it is my turn to be the backbone she needs, a hand to pull her from whatever darkness she dares to face alone. "You don't have to tell me, focus on breathing."

Her pulse beating under the pads of my fingers remains constant, even though the movements of her body have ceased.

"Listen, please. This is important."

Giving her a nod of encouragement, I mime a pretend lock over my lips, bringing forth a beautiful smile and delicate giggle. A gulp of water from a cup on her nightstand does the trick of filling out her voice, hinting at the sound of health.

"Despite being a little girl, I knew my mother was not going to get up after that fall and if she did, my father could fool anyone, giving him time to try again until she didn't. After her funeral, I suffered every night when I closed my eyes. Sleep paralysis took control over my tiny body, physically chained to my princess bed. It didn't take long until my consciousness slipped the confines of skin, astral projecting me to the realm where an entity thrived on my fear."

"Astral what? You're not making sense."

"Astral travel. I didn't believe it for the longest time, but trauma splitting from the years of abuse bisected my psyche. Only, it wasn't a peaceful journey."

"Nightmares can't hurt you Ray," I reassure her gently.

"Mine can," she rebuttals. "My whole life, I have been tormented by a creature who roams a wooded realm. Haunting me, and torturing me since childhood, all in the name of enjoyment, yet it refuses to reveal itself to me. I named the entity Ondrayus."

Bringing an arm out from underneath the comforter, she cautiously hands me the gold medallion. "I am unsure how Rebekah's family came in possession of this evil, but it destroys lives. She knew everything before she felt forced to take her life and I was too late to receive the warning in time."

Carefully taking it from her, I can't help the look of confusion contorting my facial features. I hold my breath waiting for an explanation that doesn't come.

Watching her eyes drift closed and the rise and fall of her chest slow down, she says one last thing, "You have to be the one to destroy the gateway, it has already captured my blood and invaded my mind. You are my last hope."

18

I AM GREETED BY THE FAMILIAR, DEAFENING VOID OF DARKNESS, richly saturated in grotesque decay and filth. Hidden under the protective shield of shadows lurks a vile beast set forth on a mission to destroy happiness. Rooted deeply, embedding itself in one's mind, feeding on the chaos and fear it creates. A dark, achromatic realm plaguing those who fall victim to its trap.

"Welcome back, my Queen," it announces. The unearthly tone resonates an unwelcome frigid breath along my skin. Spewed poison stinging the mind and ears.

Clenching my fists at my sides, I release a guttural, malevolent scream in all directions. "I'm not your queen! Show yourself, coward!"

The intensity of my voice bounces and echoes off the

dense fog-covered trees. My face burns red and my body fuels with scorching rage. Powerful, audible exhales surge out of my mouth with each rise and fall of my chest.

"Do you believe yourself worthy?" its raspy, taunting response reverberates back, leaving no indication of its whereabouts in this otherworld.

Unaware of the mysterious surroundings in front of me, I place all of my trust in the feet that have traversed this perilous landscape numerous times. This purgatory is his domain to control and exploit. I am the outsider here. A puppet who no longer wishes to be influenced by the villainous puppeteer.

Dried, dead leaves crunch beneath my feet as I carefully navigate my way around this lifeless aether. Noxious foreign vapor billows higher as I bring myself deeper into the void. Absent of an unobstructed path, razor-sharp twigs and underbrush slash, cut, and shred my skin, inciting sharp hissing gasps. The opaque haze alters my perception of which way I should be going, I am merely following the path guided by a lifetime of sleepless nights drenched in sweat. The strength I carry now is for the little girl inside me who didn't know she had the capability of fighting back. Fear tries and fails to infect me now.

Stiffening my spine, calm and thorough breaths balance the adrenaline building in my tissue. Curved sticks, fallen branches, and detritus of the forest floor do their best to ensnare me in their grasp, even though I am well too familiar with the trickery buried inside their nature. Pawns manipulated by their pitiless skillful master.

"Come out and face me you spineless craven!" I spit venomously.

Murderous laughter erupts around me, weaving an invisible vice grip on my body. My breathing and heart rate accelerate, whereas fear and panic simmer weakly beneath the surface. Spinning in circles to locate the son of a bitch, the shadows morph in slithering patterns, camouflaging any signs of movement.

"You know, you are not the first opponent who dares try to defeat me. That little fox was a bit too eager to throw herself on the sacrificial pyre."

"What did you do to Rebekah? She wouldn't have murdered all of those women if you weren't meddling with her mind."

"She was no match for me. Am I not entitled to a little fun?"

"NO!" I shout, straining my voice from the force put behind the word.

"It will give me great pleasure to destroy you, unless, of course, the Queen chooses to stay loyal alongside her King."

"I will do no such thing. You're nothing but a loathsome, murderous leech, doomed to rot. I've returned to make sure you stay hidden," I snarl.

Another eruption of laughter chokes the air, giving it a painful shocking prickle up my arms.

Navigating this realm is proving to be more difficult than anticipated. Devoid of a discernible direction, the sinuous knot of doubt writhes uncomfortably in my stomach. Questioning madness ensnares thoughts that I am walking in circles, progression nonexistent. The decayed debris encompassing the uneven, roughened terrain feels hollowed out under my feet and distinguishable from the rugged sections I've previously navigated. Haunted by the dread of failure, I conjure happy family images of the massacred women and force my body to persevere onward.

Halting me in place, a small clearing opens up in front of me. Thinning out, the heavy fog gradually dissipates the further inward my eyes travel. Standing directly in the center, is a mammoth-sized, otherworldly tree; a deteriorated carbon copy of the magnificent red maple where hikers discovered Rebekah's body. Its rotten, cracked, and contorted dead limbs coil outward, projecting a grim materialized presence. Under my feet I feel an anchored pulse, emanating from the exposed, cavernous roots.

Concentrating on the familiar thrum, the frightening, suffocating aura of the aether fractures from a crisp snap of a branch behind me.

"Do you remember that tree?"

The close proximity of his words induces a shudder down my spine, cementing me in place. Struggling to turn around, its words ring out in a piercing stab to my ears.

"Ondrayus."

Awaiting a response, the unsettling silence lingers intentionally on his behalf.

"Lavender," Ondrayus says. *"You smelled of lavender the evening you first visited me. Too big for that tattered teddy bear, and yet, you clutched that heinous thing in your arms. A gift from mommy dearest, I presume?"*

"Enough of this! You know nothing about me!" I scream, breaking the unseen trap holding me in place and allowing me to whip my body around to finally face my tormentor.

"I know you blame yourself. Innocently weeping and calling out for her to protect you. Pathetic," he mocks.

My eyes widen when I come face to face with him for the first time in my life. Cloaked over his entire frame is a predominately disintegrated, shredded black cloth, containing an oversized hood to conceal his face. Swallowing down bile, the acrid, putrefying malodor wafts off him, igniting a string of irrepressible retching.

Circling me like prey, I can hear the hissing sound of his nose inhaling my scent.

"Your guilt is borderline fulfilling, as is your fear of me."

"Stop this!" I yell at the shrouded face as he completes his predatorial prowl. Burying my nails into the flesh of my palms, I can feel the skin split from the pressure, trickling blood out of the half-moon slits. Burning tears of anger threaten to fall down my face.

"Reveal yourself, parasite," I demand.

Long gangly, skeletal hands creep out from beneath the shadows of his cloak. Remnants of revolting sinew cling to the rotten cinereal bones of his hands, wrists, and forearms. Unmasked by the garment, the necrotized flesh burns its rancid stench in the lining of my nasal passages. Unshrouding his head, I am unexpectedly possessed by the jarring, disfigured creature. Chunks of removed buccal tissue reveal recessed gums, bearing diseased yellow shards for teeth, and maimed jaw bones. Fissures line the residual fragments of discolored facial bones. Sunken eye sockets hold black eyes, ominously staring directly at me.

"Is that better my Queen?"

"You sicken me," I spit at him.

In one fluid motion, I brace a foot down in the dirt, spin my body around, and successfully land my other foot into his chest with a sickening thud. Hollowed resonance fills the void following the impact of the kick. Despite it only staggering him back a few feet, the question of whether or not he has a corporeal form is officially answered. Unfortunately, being plagued and emaciated isn't enough to eviscerate the chest cavity like I hoped. Receiving this information does however spark another flame inside my chest. Thoughts and tactics form potential outcomes for the fight I have willingly brought to his wasteland.

"Your pathetic attempts to defeat me are rather pitiful," Ondrayus laughs.

Taken off guard, he lunges forward, snarling incoherent rambles and spewing a red-tinged foam from his malformed, deranged mouth. Unable to move out of the way fast enough, his strength surprises me as he hooks his gaunt fingers into my shirt. Torn fabric disintegrates around his fetid, poisonous grip. Trying to avoid his wretched spray of bile, I tilt my head to the side and elongate my neck as hard as my muscles will allow. Burning wet droplets, splatter down my neck and chest from his rabid lunacy. My heart leaps to my throat in panic, doused in adrenaline. There is no time for freight, I must stand my ground and fight until this is over.

Matching arm lengths allows me to mimic the same hold on his fragmented cloak. Stinging engulfs the skin on my palms where his fabric bunches under my white-knuckled grip. Using the pain as a driving motivator, I breathe through the burn until it decreases in potency to discomfort. Digging my toes in the damp soil, I press all of my power forward, driving Ondrayus back until he collides firmly with the tree planted in the center of the clearing.

His unsightly skull bounces and cracks upon impact, sending pieces of his frontal and parietal bones to the ground, splintering further on the entangled roots beneath us. His skeletal form goes limp in my grasp. Instead of letting him fall to the ground, my fists refuse to unlock out of his cloak for fear this is another one of his skillful tricks.

A small gasp in horror leaves my mouth when my eyes travel from his chest to witness the state of the contents inhabiting his cranium. An eroding, ashen-colored brain still resides in his mangled, animated corpse. Shriveled, dead maggots lay scattered in the liquified portions of brain matter. Gouged pieces of the intact side were burrowed out by worms, centipedes, and other night crawlers. No amount of time spent around the dead can prepare you for a repulsive image such as this. Projectile vomit roars instantly out of my mouth, coats the front of mine and Ondrayus' chests, and lands with a resounding plop in the coagulated maggot-filled brain stew.

Throwing his head back, vociferous bellows of laughter bubble up his throat. Confusion scrambles my thoughts at what could be so humorous. For most of our time together in this field of death, I have had the upper hand. Frantically tossing my head around, my body starts to tremble in unfettered panic. I cannot become complacent in a realm that does not answer to me.

As the laughter builds, the movement of his hands steals my attention. Repositioning his grip on my shirt, his sharpened bones plunge into the skin of my upper chest and latch onto the top portions of my ribcage, rupturing the connection to my shoulder joints. Cracked screams of suffering permeate the area as warm, gushing blood soaks my shirt. Remnants of facial flesh barely attached to bone, contort in his own version of a sinister grin. Saliva stained a soft hue of red, drools out the corners of his mouth and chin. Gasping for air, an elongated slender black tongue extends from behind his diseased teeth and slurps at the blood spilling down my chest. Incapable of speaking, my muscles quiver as silent sobs rip me apart.

Bringing his deep-set, blackened eyes up to meet mine again, coherent, smooth words descend upon my ears. *"I warned you. I even offered you a way to stay here with me and rule by my side."*

"F-fuck you," I spit the blood-coated words on his face, speckling his grotesque bones crimson.

"You do not know when to give up do you?" Ondrayus cackles, using his cloak to smear the blood across the residual fragments of skull.

Building strength back in my voice, I find the courage needed to push forward. "I've waited a lifetime to defeat you, there is no way in hell I'm stopping now."

Taking in a deep breath, I unlatch my right hand from his cloak, reach inside my jeans pocket, and slide out a knife. Interrupting his frenzied laughter, I push down the trigger on the side of the handle to unleash a four-inch lethal blade. Swiftly seizing the moment, I reach up and slam the blade downward, connecting perfectly to his left eye. Bone chilling howls screech in agony from his demonic mouth, as black gelatinous ooze erupts down his face caused by the disastrous blow. Tearing his hands from my chest, more of my flesh and tissue are severed, inducing a quick head rush due to blood loss.

Witnessing his anguish, restored adrenaline electrifies my pained body, reawakening the motivation for sending myself to this realm. Power finds the shredded muscles of my chest and shoulder joint, briefly allowing for more movement. Taking hold of the blade's handle, a stomach-churning squelch gurgles as I jerk it out of the eye socket, stringing a line of ooze and rotten flesh off the blade. His trembling hands reach up to find remnants of the eye swimming in liquified brain matter cascading down the freshly made canal.

A deep roar rumbling within his throat is abruptly extinguished as the entire length of my blade is driven horizontally into his neck. Groans of anger morph to desperate pleas and then again to beautiful silence when the blade finishes severing slowly through the disfigured neck, embedding into the bark of the tree. The sweetest taste of victory coats my tongue watching the head of Ondrayus roll off the stump of his body and fragmentize upon impact with the ground.

Watching his headless, inanimate corpse fall in pieces

against the jagged tree roots unchains me from a lifetime of insurmountable terror when closing my eyes.

Staggering backward in the opposite direction, I stumble over fallen debris and impale myself through the torso on a broken tree stump. Mutilated flesh and pieces of severed organs hang over the jagged shards of broken wood, painting everything in close proximity a vibrant shade of red. Heaping amounts of blood spew upward into my throat, expelling a crimson fountain out of my mouth as I gasp futilely for air. The weight of my dangling flesh suit plunges the splintered wood deeper, substantially butchering my body further in half. Fibrous ropes of muscle tissue mercilessly shred as revolting snaps of torture fill the void.

Excruciating amounts of agony engulf the entirety of my being, warping my vision in a blurry haze. The soft sounds of crunching leaves steal my attention as a cloaked figure creeps toward me. A wheezing laugh of insanity breaks loose out of my punctured lungs.

"Perfection."

Acknowledgments

To my loving husband, Pluto.

To Rachel, Mikel, and YD, cross my black heart, this book would not be here without you three. I can write a story, but I am terrible at expressing the full extent of how much you mean to me. Together, you helped unwrap a part of myself I have hidden away for sixteen years. You fought for months to get me to start writing and I am beyond words grateful. From your constant reassurance, late-night chats, and unforgettable support, you have shown me the gift of true friendship. Praise the ROTD series for bringing our amazing friend group together. This one is for you. Thank you, so much for inspiring me. I love you guys.

To The Vampire Queen, Kalista, I will be forever thankful for how much you have helped me with this story. You were the first person who heard my idea for this tale and when you said you'd buy it, I knew then I had to give it a chance. Now, it may have drastically changed since that moment, but it was your inspiration that helped thrive.

To David, an amazing person that I found in the horror community, and now you're someone I get to call a friend. I can't thank you enough for pushing my wicked mind even further and entertaining the darkness forever bursting to be unleashed. Cheers to many more badass stories to release between the two of us. Also, screw the happily ever after!

To the Windsor house and its beings, thank you for the

initial inspiration that morphed the fractured idea into a full story. Thank you for listening to my never-ending list of doubts and complaints over the last few months. I'm not promising they will stop, so I hope you love the stories I have yet to unravel.

To Arianna, thank you for being the last drop in the bucket I needed to sit down and write this story. Starting is the hardest part, and you made that easy for me. I appreciate you stepping out of your comfort zone and giving my wild horror ride a chance.

To the readers who decided to give my book a chance, a massive thank you to all of you. I hope you loved this whirlwind of a story because it was extremely fun to create.

Last but not least, to my sixteen-year-old self, we fucking did it.

About The Author

Sienna Rae currently lives on the East Coast with her husband and furry creatures.

She has a neurodivergent spicy brain and makes the most out of life dealing with Ehlers-Danlos Syndrome. She finds enjoyment in the world of books and escaping within the words of a page.

Growing up, Sienna gravitated toward crime shows and horror movies, which deeply influence her writing style today. She finds enjoyment in switching things up and writing stories that don't always have the happiest of endings, so expect the unexpected.

When Sienna doesn't have her nose in a book, she can be found hiking in the woods or playing in the rain.

linktr.ee/author.sienna.rae

www.ingramcontent.com/pod-product-compliance
Lightning Source LLC
Chambersburg PA
CBHW021550310726
48972CB00003B/761